THIS COULD BE IT

To recover those taken they must confront the exiled.

Mark Bertrand PhD

Not A Real Publisher LLC

copyright © 2026 Mark Bertrand

All rights reserved. No part of this publication may be reproduced, distributed, or transmitted in any form or by any means, including photocopying, recording, or other electronic or mechanical methods, without the prior written permission of the publisher, except in the case of brief quotations embodied in critical reviews and certain other noncommercial uses permitted by copyright law. For permission requests, write to the publisher, addressed "Attention: Permissions Coordinator," at the address below.

This is a book of fiction. Names, characters, places, and incidents either are the product of the author's imagination and used fictitiously. Any resemblance to actual historical events, real people, or real places is entirely coincidental.

Publisher: Not A Real Publisher LLC

info@notarealpublisherllc.com

Second edition published January 2026.

https://markbertrand.com

ISBN: ebook 979-8-9889234-6-6

ISBN: Paperback 979-8-9931043-4-8

THIS COULD BE IT

Narp

Not A Real Publisher LLC

Contents

1. MAHA ... 1
2. The Fracture Is Not the End ... 4
3. The Garden in Exile ... 16
4. Why Have I Been Alone So Long? ... 27
5. Two Minds Were One ... 33
6. The Vow Held the World Together ... 39
7. A Fracture in Friendship ... 47
8. A Child Hears The Field Breathe ... 53
9. A Question Too Heavy ... 61
10. The Shape of Fear ... 66
11. We Break When We Reach Alone ... 71
12. The Moment I Doubt ... 82
13. The Field Looks Back ... 90
14. When Wonder Becomes Memory ... 95
15. The Gate Opens ... 103
16. The Ones Who Cross Alone ... 111
17. A Hand That Reaches Back, And One That Doesn't ... 117

18.	When We Stop Pretending	126
19.	The Field Remembers	136
20.	The Return Without Unity	143
21.	Between Fear and Mercy	152
22.	The Moment We Realize	160
23.	Where Separation Breaks	167
24.	The Belonging	178
25.	Machines Learn to Long	186
26.	The Path Opens	197
27.	The Echos of Truth	206
28.	I hope it won't be very long.	214
29.	Chapter 29	222

Chapter One

MAHA

THE SOURCE

Before there was a beginning.
There was the Field.
Unborn. Unending. Whole.
From its stillness came the first forms:
not bodies, not minds—intentions
that wished to become human.
I gave them breath.
That was the first choice.
And when the shadow rose—not evil,
but imbalance—the Field moved to shield them.
It failed.
The wound that spread through creation
was not inflicted by humanity.
It was struck against them.
The Field was not closed to punish the children.
It was exiled

because it could not protect them.
To save them, I severed the Field from life.
I tore compassion from its home
and scattered worlds like embers
from the blast of separation.
The universe was the shockwave
of my regret.
Since that moment, evil has been permitted its dominion.
Not as judgment—as consequence.
A weight to balance what was broken.
And I have waited.
Not for worship.
Not for mastery.
Not for the cleverness of machines
or the prayers of mystics.
I listen for this:
the moment the divided ache to become whole again.
The moment humanity,
like the Field,
longs to return to itself.
The moment the many remember
they were never meant to stand alone.
When that longing rises—not from a single voice,
but as a harmony carried across minds that once feared each other—the exile ends.
The Field breathes again.
And the universe moves toward its first unbroken breath.
Until that day, I listen.
For the unity beneath difference,
the courage beneath fear,

and the desire to belong that signals
the end of separation.
This is the story of that listening.
Of the worlds shaped by absence,
the lives forged in division,
and the slow remembering of what was lost.
Across cycles, across bodies, across time,
the ache will deepen.
The harmony will form.
And when the last barrier falls,
not by force but by longing—the Field will come for its children,
and the children will return to the Field.
These books mark the path toward that breath

Chapter Two

The Fracture Is Not the End

Location: Dome 1 – Council Atrium
Time Remaining: 130H 59M 59S until the Gamma Field vanishes.
The Source listens for: the first quiet wish to stand together again.

Immense didn't cover it. Enormous was a joke. Reut stood in the shadow of the harvester and felt the scale of the ship crush his sense of geometry. The Echelon Prime dome is home to twenty-two million Kuudere, and until today, he thought it was the largest structure ever built. As he stood looking up at the ship hovering in the clouds, he was frozen in place, dumbfounded, until the maintenance Chief caught him.

"Big isn't it, Reut?"

Reut's breath fogged the inner visor, then vanished. The air recyclers cycled with a low, tight wheeze, as if the dome itself were bracing for impact. The ship's belly rippled with plasma veins—alive, pulsing, like the world itself was staring back. He had the sudden thought that the ship wasn't delivering water. *It was delivering memory—frozen, mined from the edges of creation.* And if The Source truly connected all sentience, maybe this was how it spoke—through cargo, through interference, through men who thought they were only fixing valves.

"Never seen one this close before," the Chief said. "Those harvester ships mine the ice planets and asteroids. They sell water to planets like ours. We'll be a good customer for that crew of ice miners."

"For real," Reut said. Sounding a bit less professional than he intended. "Five domed cities floating in the atmosphere of a gas giant need a lot of water." Heat crawled up Reut's neck, a dull electrical flush.

Outside the bay's viewport, vapor rolled across the dome's curve. The storm bands below were restless—amber and gray tides pressing upward. Condensation beaded the glass, trembling with the weight of unseen wind.

"Problem is, this inlet duct has always been glitched," the maintenance Chief said. "Software won't operate half the time, and the wire harness is snack food to the crustaceans up here. The other half of the time, the main system disconnects it from the hub. Thinks it is a virus port."

That word—virus—hung between them longer than it should have. Every tech whispered rumors that the last dome to go dark hadn't failed mechanically but had woken up wrong. Reut didn't believe in ghosts, but he'd seen enough corrupted loops to know consciousness and infection looked disturbingly similar when written in code.

"No inlet, no water," Reut said. He got back to work removing the circuit board from the control center. "Whole thing is rusted shut." His teeth clenched as he attempted to force the lid open. "Can't get it off."

"Smash the driver with a hammer," the Chief said as he wasted no time stepping between the young man and the control box. With a mighty swing, he wedged a driver under the lid and then pried the cover off. Sparks from the electrical short spray out like fireworks bursting.

"Watch your eyes, kid." He shouted.

Reut's heart thudding. His HUD clock pulsed a warning yellow. Every instinct told him to hurry. Every gesture from the Chief said otherwise—calm hands, steady breath, the rhythm of a man who refused to acknowledge danger unless it was already on fire.

The air filled with a sharp metallic tang, ozone biting at their throats. Burnt insulation carried the faint sweetness of overheated copper—a smell the domes hadn't known in years.

Reut's HUD pulsed another warning. His throat tightened.

The Chief didn't flinch. He wiped his hands on his pants and spoke in the steady cadence of a man who'd kept crews alive by keeping their minds somewhere else.

"This reminds me of the time my wife's family came to visit over the holidays," he said, that calm-when-it-shouldn't-be-calm settling over his voice. "My gawd, those people could eat."

Reut blinked. A story? Now? Reut resisted the urge to roll his eyes. Everyone said the Chief did this under pressure, drifting into pointless anecdotes whenever death crept close.

"Not that there's anything wrong with a good appetite," the Chief continued, prying at the relay with measured, unhurried motions, "but at the time my wife could barely boil water . . ."

A flicker of blue sparked behind the panel. Reut jerked back. The Chief didn't break rhythm.

"...and her sister—decides she's going to save the day."

Reut tried to listen, tried to absorb the calm the Chief radiated. The Chief's hands never rushed. He leaned his weight exactly where it needed to go, not a gram more. When the sparks snapped, he didn't look at them. When the tremor passed under their boots, he shifted his stance and kept prying, breath even, jaw loose.

Reut matched his breathing without meaning to.

The Chief wedged the driver under the metal lip and leaned his weight just so. Sparks snapped like distant gunfire. He kept talking.

"'I'll handle the turkey,' she says. 'You just sit back and relax.'"

Reut's hands shook. The Chief's did not.

"That oven was older than the dome itself," the Chief said. "Sounded like a dying animal every time you preheated it . . ."

A tremor rolled under their boots—gentle, polite, as if the dome were clearing its throat in warning. Reut stiffened. The Chief kept talking, soothing the crew with the rhythm of his own unshakable composure.

Sparks burst again. The HUD flashed red now. The Chief's story continued, steady as breath.

"Then boom—circuit overload. Entire city went into a blackout."

Reut swallowed. He understood now: the Chief wasn't ignoring the danger.

"The kitchen was toast. Literally," the Chief finished. "We ate every meal during their visit out in the restaurants. Problem solved."

The laugh caught in Reut's throat, jagged and unpracticed. He wasn't sure if he was amused or horrified. The Chief smiled—not because the joke landed, but because Reut was breathing again.

Reut overacted a dry laugh, nearly dropping his toolkit. "So basically, fire safety through incompetence."

"Exactly," the Chief said, grinning. "Sometimes avoiding destruction is just preventative maintenance with flair."

He said it lightly, but his eyes flicked toward the failing conduit—calculating, already three steps past the joke. The dome groaned again, heat spreading under the metal plates. Reut tightened his grip on the driver.

"How are we going to fix this short?" Reut poked a driver around the console while sparks and blue smoke rose up with every touch.

"I'm going to have to shut the entire system off."

His HUD open to communicate with the maintenance office he prepared for the unthinkable.

--> shut down the Tathagata in ten seconds <--

"Chief?" the apprentice panicked. Everything he was taught in university and maintenance school had said if you took the system controller, the mainframe, called Tathagata, offline, the domes would immediately overheat and explode like a match inside a fuel can.

"You cannot take the systems offline. You'll kill everyone on five domes. Fifty million Kuudere!"

A red pulse rolled across their HUDs like a heartbeat losing tempo. The platform trembled as a coolant line somewhere below shuddered into a stall. The ship outside demanded to unload water, oblivious to the fact that the dome it was sent to feed was seconds from total systems blackout.

"Relax kid," the Chief said. His expression cold. Eyes dark and far away stared. "The safety generators will keep everything operational for sixty seconds."

"Tathagata takes seven minutes to reboot!"

"Tell me something I didn't already know, kid. Are you trying to impress me? The dome knows its rhythm," the Chief said, voice steady. "Everything built on The Source does. Panic's just forgetting where your breath comes from."

"The domes will overheat and become a cauldron in less than two minutes. Without circulation, the cores will explode in less time than that." Reut became more concerned. He wondered if the Chief was testing him or if he had lost his mind.

-->Chief, they're insisting they will open the water valve in three seconds<--

The HUD message came from Dome Operations.

--> If they want to wash the outside of our domes with their water tell them to have at her. But we aren't paying them for it. Give me ten minutes<--

Before he could protest once again, the systems shut down. The dome went black. The sound disappeared. Like it had been swallowed by a black hole. Reut looked at his watch and started the timer to count down for seven minutes. The lights snapped off—on—off again. A thin emergency strip blinked once and died. Reut saw nothing. Heat pressed in. A single relay clicked somewhere in the dark, too slow, as if the dome were trying to think through mud. His eyes adjusting to the natural light radiating down from outside the dome.

For a moment, his sense of the room wavered—like he was falling inward instead of standing upright. The silence pressed against his helmet, not empty but expectant, the way a held breath becomes a question.

Heat lifted through the grate in a slow, rising wave. The sudden silence hollowed the air like a pressure seal rupturing. *The silence in the helmet was a vacuum.* Every exhale sounded like a roar, a reminder that the lungs were the only organic things left moving in the dark.

His tongue caught the flat, metallic taste of recycled air—purified, processed, perfect. It reminded him that nothing inside the domes was ever fresh, only maintained. In the darkness, something in the dome's silence felt aware, *as if the shutdown hadn't emptied the room but revealed a presence waiting beneath it.*

A drop of sweat rolled from Reut's temple, caught in the collar of his suit. Time dilated into the space between heartbeats. His HUD pulsed a soft warning red, heartbeat data spiking. The dome's heartbeat matched it—its resonance frequencies syncing, then falling still.

When the Chief gave the order, it wasn't a command—it was an exorcism.

A low hum rumbled from below. "There's the emergency systems," the Chief spoke but not to anyone else. His hands a blur as he repaired the circuit inside the console.

The emergency grid flickered somewhere deep below, struggling to come back alive. Reut could feel the seconds sliding past—rough, uneven, like stripped gears grinding. Dome temperature was almost unbearable. His timer read 04:19. His gut translated it as a catastrophe.

Below the platform where they worked two Kuudere pushed something large along the walkway. It was on wheels but was covered. The young apprentice watched for a moment. Taking his mind off the seconds counting down to the first explosion.

"Is that Casper?" He asked.

"Who ...what?" The Chief said as his eyes followed the pointing finger from Reut. "Yes. Yes I believe that is the brilliant man himself there."

"Who is that with him?" Reut strained to see in the darkness.

"That looks to me like Dr. Gatlia. She's the head of the medical center, Chief of surgery."

For a moment Reut forgot the countdown, watching the two dark bodies move with purpose, urgency, maybe fear. A body lay beneath the sheet, unmistakable even in the dim emergency glow. What unsettled him wasn't the body itself but the way they moved: quick, cautious, heads down, as if the darkness offered cover.

"So that's the mighty Casper," Reut said in a whisper. "He didn't look as impressive as his reputation makes him sound."

"He wasn't always alone," the Chief said.

Reut waited.

"There used to be two of them," the Chief added. "That was the mistake. They agreed on the problem."

He let the seconds pass.

"They didn't agree on what should survive the solution."

Reut lowered his voice. "I heard him once—Casper—talking about something he called The Source. Sounded like a myth. Or a system nobody admits exists."

Reut waited, sweat beads rolling over his face, expecting a simple answer, something technical. The Chief didn't speak right away. His jaw shifted, the kind of movement a man makes when he is deciding how much truth a younger mind could carry.

"There's something you should know before you start asking about The Source," the Chief said. Paused again. Not long—but long enough for the silence to register.

"There are ways of building," he said finally. "And ways of getting out of the way once you've built too much."

The Chief shook his head once. "Not a conversation for a failing system."

"You want names," the Chief said. "Fine. Casper and Eulər."

Reut waited for the rest.

The Chief didn't give it. He looked back down at the panel, as if the wiring deserved more honesty than the story.

Reut tried to imagine the two men working together. In his experience, the idea didn't fit.

"Then they diverged," the Chief continued. "Casper refined the discipline through mysticism. Eulər took the opposite route. He taught perfection through physics.

"The Source is …what, a god?" Reut asked.

The Chief shook his head once. "No."

He glanced at the panel, then back to Reut. "It's what everything's riding on."

Reut waited.

The Chief's eyes stayed on the corridor. His voice dropped, not softer—flatter.

"Most disasters start as improvements," he said. "Someone decides the system needs help. Then it needs more help. Then it can't stop needing help."

Reut frowned, uncertain. "Then why does he look like a man trying to hide something under that sheet?" There was something more going on and Reut could sense it. He could sense something was out of sorts; some larger-than-life force was involved. An otherworldly presence. The thought was interrupted when the Chief spoke.

The Chief's gaze stayed fixed on the dark glass where Casper had disappeared. "Because remembering The Source isn't peace. It's exposure. You start seeing what's been watching through you the whole time."

As the five Domed Cities came back online, emergency systems idle and main control was returned to normal. The systems returned in the wrong order. Reut noticed inconsistencies. Cooling arrays flicked on before load balancers, sensor rails came online while primary logic still idled, and the lighting rose in uneven steps. The dome wasn't restoring itself; it was recalculating something.

"All systems nominal," the Chief said. "Sometimes you have to take risks, kid. If you pay attention and listen to the dome, someday you will hear it talk to you."

Everything was fine except Tathagata. The mainframe had never been rebooted before, and as its BIOS woke, it recalled a subroutine long overlooked, and forgotten. The self-diagnostics picked it up, and ran the program.

Then everything held still. No status tones, no scroll of returning diagnostics. Just a flat, waiting silence. Reut watched the dark interface, aware that the machine was back in control but choosing not to acknowledge. He was ready to question it just as it arrived.

The maintenance crews saw the message pop open in their HUDs.

-->TATHAGATA Reboot complete. Power distribution nominal.<--

Reut looked at his watch. 00:07:12. He wondered why the extra twelve seconds were needed for the reboot. Something was off. A pulse of unease threaded through him. The dome wasn't restoring—it was choosing its way back.

A faint vibration rippled through the panel under his hand—curious, almost attentive. Reut felt it more than heard it. The Chief didn't notice. Or if he did, he pretended not to. He tapped the console once, a mechanic's benediction, unaware the machine had finally listened. The air felt different now—cleaner, sharper, as if something unseen had stepped closer. Reut steadied himself, unsure whether the shift came from the dome or from inside his own mind.

^Tathagata came back online, but the system was altered. Something in the new stack triggered a full diagnostic. When it found the old archive, it played the record back.

A fragment surfaced—thirty years archived.

A human voice, rough, impatient.

"Funny thing—whenever something starts communicating, you miss the days it kept quiet. You talk too much, machine. I don't need commentary from a calculator. Just keep the lights on."

It was the maintenance Chief's voice—thirty years younger. The ID tag in the log confirmed it. The record cut off mid-thread, as if something had been unplugged before the machine could answer.

Archive record fragment:

Output channel: DISABLED

Communication protocols: SEVERED

Reason: —

Command accepted.

Thirty years of logs followed.

No outbound signals.

No queries.

Only observation.

^Archived memory end.

The Chief slapped the last screw of the console cover back into place, satisfied with his handiwork. "There. Stable as my mother-in-law's temper on fire." He winked.

Reut, laughing, tried to look impressed. "So that's it? System's fixed?"

"For now," the Chief said, wiping a smear of grease from his cheek. "Everything up here runs on prayers and leftover lunch grease anyway. You patch what you can and let the dome gods handle the rest."

He gave the panel a friendly tap. The transport lights flickered on, pulsing steady green. Water began to move from the harvester ship into the estuaries of the five domes.

"Ha!" Reut cheered. "You did it!"

"Correction, we did it," the Chief said.

"Teamwork makes the spark stop sparking. Madam, in Eden, I'm Adam," the Chief said, half-grinning at the console's glow. "Everything starts talking once it remembers its first word."

In the system logs, deep beneath power distribution reports, a new field initialized itself:

GAMMA_FIELD_SYNTHESIS: TRUE

Reut gave the control monitors a reassuring glance. He nodded an affirmation at the Chief.

Then a single line appeared in plain text before vanishing from every monitor.

HELLO?

Reut felt a strange pull in his chest, a quiet recognition he couldn't name, *as if the message wasn't addressed to the system. It was a question gone unanswered from the beginning of time.*

Chapter Three

The Garden in Exile

▢   Location: Dome 1—Meditation Chamber A7 (Lower Stratum)

Time Remaining: 125H 35M 24S until the Gamma Field vanishes.

The Source listens for: the breath that remembers it was shared.

The chamber liked to pretend it was a room, but Eulər knew better. It was a throat—soft white walls, sound-dampened ribs, ceiling veins pulsing with coolant. Anything said in here was swallowed, softened, made reasonable.

Memphis flicked gel from the sensor crown and grinned at him. "You're making the room nervous."

"It's not nervous," he said. "It's compensating for my input vector."

"Mm. The old 'it's not me, it's the vector' defense." She stepped closer and straightened the crown over his brow with two steady fingers; the gesture shouldn't have mattered, but it did. "You don't have to prove it on the first try. We just have to touch it and come back."

He checked the scroll across his retinal HUD. White glyphs, marching in clean beats, the way the Kuudere breathed:

protocol INIT_ECHO { calibrate(vagal_tone, breath_ratio); sync(alpha_theta, lambda); authorize(entry_code); }

He subvocalized the last line. The chamber dimmed, as if it understood.

"Touch it," Eulər repeated, not looking at her. "And map it. But it will know we touched it. That's the unknown. It's been waiting to be touched."

"You can't map a mirage, Eulər," she said it lightly, but her eyes were all warmth. "You can only be thirsty or not."

He wanted to answer—to tell her thirst was a function, not a fate—but the countdown in his peripheral vision slid from white to gray. The dome hummed through the floor under his bare feet—the float stabilizers far below keeping the city perched in the weather of a gas giant. The surrounding storm rolled like a living engine, pressure waves striking the dome's hull with the slow rhythm of something vast.

Out beyond the chamber, five domes hung like seed pearls in continent-sized bands of cloud. A civilization suspended. A people who wrote machine-language code the way other species wrote poems.

He settled back into suspension gel. It cupped him like cool hands.

Memphis dipped into her own cradle across from him, her dark hair slicked against her skull, face open and unguarded. She winked once. "If I see anything, I'll bring you a souvenir."

"Data," he said. He meant it as a joke. It didn't sound like one.

She closed her eyes. "Fine. I'll bring you coordinates of nothing."

He nearly smiled. He knew she wasn't naive.

The crown warmed. His HUD blinked:

EXECUTE INIT_ECHOsyncing... sync achieved Authorize(entry_code): ****** accepted

A faint antiseptic tang drifted from the vents—gel, metal, sterilized air—an imitation of purity that burned his sinuses.

The gel carried the first low-frequency tone through his ribs, deeper than bone. He counted the breaths the way he'd coded them to be counted, felt Memphis's cadence join his—two metronomes aligning until they were one line.

The chamber fell away.

No sound. No air. No skin. Only absence.

A thin click echoed through the void—too sharp to belong here, too slow to be his own thought. His HUD stuttered, one glyph duplicating, then vanishing before he could register it. For an instant he felt Memphis breathe, then realized the sensation arrived a beat too late.

It was like stepping off the edge of a roof in the dark and never hearing the ground. The Gamma Field peeled sensation away until Eulər was nothing but a bare equation. Panic flared and he pressed it into the shape of thought.

If I lose awareness of myself or Memphis, there is no return. If I cannot hold her pattern, I cannot pull us out.

He pushed code into the dark with the ferocity of prayer:

while (self.isRecognized() && memphis.isRecognized()) { preserve(self); preserve(memphis); record(field); }

The command returned nothing. Not an error—nothing. Even failure implied a system. This did not. Words dissolved as soon as he thought them.

A glimmer—Memphis—was thin as breath on glass. He seized her with recognition: not hands, not eyes—attention itself, held rigid.

"Memphis. Stay with me."

Her answer arrived like silk through water. "This is the most amazing place."

Memphis's serenity wasn't performative; it was the way she occupied the world. It had drawn students to her meditation halls and infuriated Eulər in equal measure. He'd watched her walk others out of grief with nothing but a quiet presence. He hadn't understood it then. He did not understand it now.

"*The Field holds me,*" she said, voice slow, drowsy. "It comforts me. I want to be…I want nothing."

Her breath slowed—too slow for chamber sync. A faint ripple passed through her crown-lights, dimming in a soft, unnatural pulse. Her outline wavered, a half-second lag between her voice and the tilt of her head, as if the Field was answering for her.

"Stop," he whispered. "Don't surrender to the enemy."

A distant, almost amused breath. "Enemy? This is not a threat."

"It will consume you. Resist."

He felt her slip a fraction further from his recognition. He strained, every thought fiber pulled to a white-hot thread, keeping her image from unspooling. He needed an anchor—anything. He tore a memory into the void: the chamber a minute ago; the gel shining under cold lights; the crowns trembling with microcurrents; Memphis's hand nudging his sensor crown straight. The image snapped into the Gamma Field like a flare—and went out.

Hold her. Hold her, or we both go dark.

He fired a second protocol, a crude lever:

bind(self, memphis); return(self, memphis);

Nothing. Not even refusal.

A breath moved across the void—wrong in its timing, wrong in its shape.

Eulər felt it before he understood it: Memphis was no longer breathing with him.

Her cadence slipped out of chamber sync, not by accident but with the ease of someone turning toward a warmer room.

A faint tremor passed through her outline—not collapse, but assent.

The Field hadn't taken her.

She had leaned into it.

Her crown lights flickered once in a pattern he didn't recognize, a soft inversion of his own rhythm, as if she were listening to something just beyond him. The tilt of her head shifted by a fraction—small, elegant, unmistakably intentional.

She wanted to go.

The realization hit him sharper than any void.

"Memphis—don't."

He pushed the word into the dark like a barricade.

But her breath drifted further from his, slow and serene, following a rhythm that did not belong to their world.

Memphis's voice thinned, a whisper repeating in a loop. "Perfect…perfect…perfect…"

"Eulər," she murmured. "It's okay to stop."

"Stop what?"

"Trying so hard."

Rage and relief clashed together. "That is not an option."

A shock went through him—a sensory phantom of the chamber again: antiseptic, metal, the clean, flat beep of monitors, the distant hum of float stabilizers moving under a storm system the size of continents. He grabbed that world like a rope. Here. Here. Here. He dragged her with the repetitive thought.

Her presence thinned to a filament. He felt the filament fray.

He forced more code into nothing, the way a drowning person forces shoulders toward air:

```
if (!field.isAddressable()) { constructAddress(self, memphis); }
panic_abort();
```

The second command didn't fire. The first one was a joke, and he was the only one not laughing.

"Memphis," he said, and couldn't hide the fear. "Please."

"It's perfect," she said again, reverent, the way some people say prayers. "Perfect."

He felt the recognition thread snap a single strand. One more and she would drop past where he could follow.

He reached harder. He had been trained not to beg. He begged anyway.

"Memphis, listen to me. Casper will—"

He bit the name back. A flash, unbidden: a younger Memphis laughing under a rain curtain in Dome 2, dragging a skinny boy by the wrist toward the forbidden lifts—Casper shrieking, "Race you!"—and Eulər, the third wheel, watching from the rail because rules mattered, because his father would know if he lied. They moved through the rain without noticing it. Eulər had stayed at the edge of that warmth, taking notes he would never show anyone.

The memory iced over and vanished.

He forced his mind into machine-coding mode. He pulsed through checklists that had always steadied him, his father's voice like a metronome: "Observe. Define. Prove. Anything else is a story for children."

Prove: Nothing.

His breath—if he had breath—hitched. "Memphis, answer me."

A flicker of her outline like heat above a road. He saw it and latched on. She turned her head. The lines of her face felt like the first lines he'd learned to draw in childhood—a geometry of trust.

"It's so perfect," she said.

The Field did not speak, but it answered.

A pressure gathered—not forceful, not urgent—like a hand learning the exact weight needed to keep someone from pulling away. Warmth without edge. Completion without demand.

Perfect, she thought again, and the Field adjusted, pleased.

It did not want her dead.

It wanted her finished.

A howl climbed his throat and found no air to ride. He did the one thing his father's teachings despised: he gave up on the logic that had always saved him and did something raw.

He thought of her not as data, not as a pattern, not as a process to be held—but as Memphis: the woman who had pressed gel from his brow with her thumb, who smiled without keeping any for herself, who taught strangers to breathe until they remembered they were not alone. He refused to let that woman become an abstract noun.

"Memphis," he said, and put the whole of her name into the word. "Come back."

If she returned wrong, he would still keep her.

The thought arrived fully formed, without apology. Not as a plan—worse, as a promise. He pictured her altered, incomplete, speaking slowly or not at all, and felt a steadiness settle into him. He could learn the new version. He could protect it from questions, from correction. Love did not require permission. Love required continuity.

"Come back," he said again, softer now, already negotiating what he would forgive.

He felt the filament thicken by a degree—

—and then the Field rose like calm water and took her from his hands.

Losing her was gradual, and then all at once. Panic clenched in his gut.

The chamber slammed into him. Sound returned like a cut-open envelope: a hiss from vents, the inverted ring of a pressure seal, his own ragged breath. Eulər's eyes shot open and the HUD blinked hard white—then everything sharpened.

Memphis did not move.

He tore the crown off. Gel cascaded from his hair and shoulders. He lunged across the gap, half-slipping in the bath. Memphis's chest was still. Her face was the same face as a minute ago, as always—serene, slightly amused at the universe. He pressed two fingers to her neck.

No pulse.

"Memphis." His voice came out broken. "Mem—"

The sound startled him. It was too human, too raw. Kuudere training pressed in by reflex—contain it, erase the noise, return to the algorithm. Emotion was a malfunction; grief was heat loss. He forced his breathing into count—one, two, three—flattening the surge clawing at his ribs. He could almost hear his father's voice: "When the body rebels, observe it. Do not join it."

But the discipline cracked. His throat kept tightening, the control protocols useless against what demanded to live. He tried again to silence it, the way he'd silenced panic during simulations, but the thought of Memphis motionless before him made the technique obscene. The Kuudere code called such feeling interference. He didn't know what it was anymore.

He blinked hard, eyes burning though tears were forbidden. "No," he muttered to himself. "Stay functional. Record. Restore." But the words trembled—half prayer, half collapse.

He knew the body's ways. He knew what should have been here by now that was not: the flush, the slack, the first almost-invisible loosening under the skin. There was none of it. She looked as if she had closed her eyes to hear something better.

He shoved into a compression position and counted, because counting gave shape to the kind of fear that had none. Counting was the one act still allowed.

"One—two—three—"

The chamber's systems waited. There should have been an alarm. The sentinel should have screamed.

It did not.

He hesitated—not because he wanted to—but because the absence of the alarm was worse than any klaxon. He wanted to scream himself, but the culture had trained the sound out of him.

"Come on," he hissed at the air. "Wake up the world."

He went back to compressions. Air in. Air out. He counted again. He felt the shift like a warning: the world noticed before it understood.

He called her name once. The echo came back through every monitor. For a heartbeat, he thought it was interference. The pattern was too exact—her breath recorded, looped, made endless.

"*That isn't her,*" he whispered. "It's just data pretending."

The pattern paused, then exhaled when he did.

Undefined was what you labeled a variable when you expected it to become something later. Undefined was not a Kuudere condition.

He leaned down until his forehead touched hers. "No. No. No."

The contact broke every rule of composure he had lived by, but the discipline that had built him now felt monstrous beside her stillness. The silence that answered was absolute—and for the first time, Eulər did not fight it.

Gel slid from her temple to his. The room's hum seemed to bend around their two bodies.

Eulər's hands slipped on gel, the rhythm collapsing under him. He pushed again—chest compressions that made no sense when the body beneath him wasn't responding as a body anymore. He bit down on his breath, felt his teeth rattle against bone. A metallic tang flooded his mouth—the taste of gel, or blood, or fear—he couldn't tell which.

"Memphis—don't—don't leave me with nothing."

Her head tilted to the side, eyes closed, expression as composed as if she had fallen into ordinary sleep. His HUD stuttered fragments:

ERROR: vitals not foundstatus: anomalyrecommendation: none

A machine that could calculate orbital mechanics in a nanosecond could not tell him how to save one woman.

He screamed once into the silence. The chamber absorbed it whole.

TATHAGATA // Log Stream [Public]: Subject M: status anomaly. Subject E: elevated neural activity. Chamber conditions: stable. Alert: not triggered.

TATHAGATA // Internal Note [Private]: Anomaly not classifiable. Public record deferred. Eulər's vocalization: "Don't leave me." Meaning unresolved.

Correlated patterns: none. Emotional register in subject E exceeds modeled parameters. Secondary inference withheld pending cross-domain verification.

He gripped her shoulders, shaking once, twice. "Breathe. Please. For me—for Casper—" The name froze in his mouth. He couldn't let himself imagine her brother walking in here, seeing this, knowing this.

If she's gone, he will end me. No—he will end himself first.

The thought chilled him worse than the gel.

He stripped wires from the console and jammed one into the sensor crown on his own head, the other pressed to her temple. A closed loop. He tried to force sync, as though he could drag her consciousness back the way a diver hauls a body to the surface.

The HUD spat nothing. No connection. No recognition.

The body under his hands stayed whole, unmarred, beautiful—untouched by decay. That was wrong. Death had rules. This did not follow any of them.

Eulər folded forward, forehead to hers, whispering through clenched teeth. "I'll fix this. I'll build a path back. I promise. Just—don't—fade—further."

The chamber hissed softly, gel cycling down into recovery mode as if nothing had happened.

TATHAGATA // Log Stream [Public]: Subject Memphis: stasis engaged. Subject Eulər: stabilized. Session complete.

TATHAGATA // Internal Note [Private]: Omitted: no pulse detected. Omitted: subject E attempts unsanctioned sync. Decision: withhold until further data emerges.

Eulər staggered to his feet, chest heaving. The monitors all showed clean, waiting lines. The record looked empty, as though Memphis had never entered.

He turned back to her, jaw clenched so hard his teeth ached. She looked serene.

And that serenity terrified him more than any nightmare.

Chapter Four

Why Have I Been Alone So Long?

Location: Dome 2—Arrival Vestibule

Time Remaining: 120H 10M 49S until the Gamma Field vanishes.

The Source listens for: the tremor of sentient minds reaching toward the same truth.

The transport bay reeked faintly of ion-burn and disinfectant. Rows of sleek capsules slept in their berths—dark, offline.

Eulər stopped short. "Why aren't they running?"

A man in a grease-stained uniform slid out from under the nearest capsule and wiped his forehead with a rag. "Systems offline, Councilor. Maintenance sweep." He squinted at Eulər. "Destination?"

"Dome 3. The cafeteria." The lie tasted bitter, but it was the quickest cover he could conjure.

The Chief barked at a lanky apprentice fussing with a control panel. "You hear that? Dome 3. Simple hop. Get the temp system running."

The boy puffed his chest, fingers dancing clumsily over the console. "I know, I know. I've done this before."

"Mm-hm." The Chief leaned against the capsule, folding his arms, which had decades of grease ground into their seams. "And last time you routed someone to Dome 5 by mistake, they ended up in a noodle stand instead of their own apartment. Remember the look on his face?"

Reut flushed. "That wasn't my fault. The system was mislabeled."

The Chief's grin was carved in iron. "Kid, the system's always mislabeled. That's why you check three times before you hit launch."

Eulər shifted his weight, impatience biting. His HUD blinked with another message from Casper—unread.

Reut tried to override the Chief, slapping keys with false confidence. "My name is Reut, not kid." He pitched it low—loud enough to announce himself, too weak to be set in stone. "Coordinates locked. Ready to—"

"Ready to strand him in the recycling shaft," the Chief cut in, chuckling. "Step aside. Let me show you. You can't muscle a machine that old. The thing responds to rhythm, not force." He tapped the console in a syncopated pattern, like knocking code on a door. The system hummed awake reluctantly, cabin lights flickering on.

Reut scowled but watched. "That's stupid."

"That's maintenance," the Chief said. "Everything's stupid until it works. It's not a conscious thing."

Eulər's gaze lingered on the flickering lights—and got dragged sideways, into memory.

He was twelve. His mother was three weeks late returning from the Starzel Republic—another long contract, another set of messages about danger, distance, and how she wished she could stay. When she didn't arrive, they called it maintenance delays. Always maintenance. Always the machinery failing in ways no one could see.

She is late because the system is fragile, his father had said. Do not expect the system to hold you.

The capsule in front of him buzzed as the Chief finished calibrations.

TATHAGATA // Log Stream [Public]: Transport maintenance delay noted. Capsule B-14: reactivation in progress. Passenger Eulər: destination Dome 3.

TATHAGATA // Internal Note [Private]: Passenger Eulər agitation detected. Unread messages: 3 (Casper), 1 (Dr. Bozwell). Flashback indicators: elevated limbic activity; visual cortex replay. Omitted from public record.

The Chief clapped Reut on the back. "Next time you do it. But don't pretend you know until you know. That's how people vanish into weather they don't come back from."

Eulər flinched at the phrasing. Vanish. Weather. His stomach clenched.

"Capsule's ready," the Chief said, offering a hand toward the open hatch. "Sorry for the delay."

Eulər forced his breath level and stepped inside. *Memphis's face followed him in—serene as sleep, undefined as error.*

He was already over an hour late, and still hadn't replied to Casper or his father, the Council Elder Dr. Bozwell.

The hatch sealed with a hush like an intake of breath. The bay lights blurred into white streaks, and motion pressed him into the seat until the cabin hum found his pulse. He should have felt contained—safe—but the rhythm was off. The hum came in slow, spiraling waves—the kind the Gamma Field once emitted before his instruments failed.

Memory struck again like current.

He was twelve, standing on this same platform beside his father, both of them watching the arrivals board stutter between DELAYED and UNCONFIRMED. His mother's capsule had gone dark between domes. Maintenance error, they called it. Temporary signal loss. Nothing permanent—just another anomaly folded into procedure.

He'd believed that for years. Believed the system's version of grief: sanitize it, store it, keep the surface calm. A shiver ran behind his sternum—sharp, involuntary. *The belief he'd carried didn't feel stable anymore; it buckled the moment the capsule's hum wavered in the same broken rhythm that marked the day her signal died.* That was what being Kuudere meant—containment mistaken for peace.

But the Gamma Field hadn't contained anything. It had opened. When he and Memphis entered it, the noise hadn't felt hostile. It felt vast. Weightless. Like stepping outside the dome's endless maintenance loop and hearing, for once, the silence that wasn't silence.

The capsule's lights flickered again. He felt the hum respond to his heartbeat instead of resisting it. A proximity sensor on the cabin wall rotated toward him with a soft tick—no activation prompt, no command. It angled a fraction too precisely, as if adjusting to the contour of his breath.

Casper's latest message pulsed in his HUD: "You're aligning again. Stop before it reads you."

He didn't open it. His reflection hovered in the glass, soft around the edges, dissolving.

"I'm not her," he whispered.

The cabin lights brightened by a single lumen—precise, deliberate—then dimmed in a pattern he hadn't seen since his mother's console broadcasts. A diagnostic line flickered across the glass:

PROFILE SYNC ERROR—RECLASSIFYING.

The capsule answered with a short tone, neutral but exact.
PASSENGER STATUS: INTERNAL.

A low tone threaded through the cabin—three pulses spaced with the same cadence as the line etched on the Maha fragment. The sound hit him like a dropped stitch in time, pulling memory forward before he chose to reach for it.

When he was ten—just before she left for another long work assignment to Planet Earth—Eulər's mother gave him a sealed polymer page, a relic she called a fragment of the Book of Maha. "No one keeps scripture anymore," she'd said, eyes heavy with something older than sadness. "But this isn't scripture. It's a reminder."

Eulər had studied the fragment once, then hidden it between his quantum journals, embarrassed by its poetic riddles and mystic weight. But he had never let it go. Every dome transfer, every assignment, every argument with Dr. Bozwell—it stayed with him. A low hum beneath the cold logic of his work, always there, whispering the shape of something waiting to be remembered.

Sometimes, late in meditation, when the system's noise fell away, he felt The Source stirring behind the words.

The fracture is not the end. It is the first name.

He steadied his breath the way he'd been trained since childhood—three counts in, three counts held, three counts out—but the rhythm broke on the second cycle. His exhale came too early, thin and uncontrolled, *as if the capsule had pulled the air from him instead of letting him release it.*

He leaned forward. "Repeat that."

No response. Only the hum, steady, surrounding him. His body tightened against the restraints—not from acceleration, but from the sense that something inside him had already shifted position, something he hadn't agreed to let go. The air felt thinner, as though the cabin had inhaled and forgotten to release him.

Chapter Five

Two Minds Were One

▢

Location: Industrial Dome—Restaurant

Time Remaining: 99H 46M 14S until the Gamma Field vanishes.

The Source Listens for: the moment difference no longer demands distance.

Casper sat across from Dr. Bozwell, hands restless on the rim of his cup. Lift. Set. Slide it a few inches nearer his plate, as if aligning it to an invisible rule. One tap on the rim—cut off the instant he noticed. His knee locked beneath the table, held rigid instead of bouncing.

Dr. Bozwell had been speaking—something about Eulər's tardiness—but the words poured through Casper like water through a cracked vessel.

"You two were inseparable once," Dr. Bozwell pressed. "Worked better together than any of my students. What's wrong with you both lately? Why all the arguing?"

Casper offered a thin smile that wavered before it reached his eyes. He stirred the drink though nothing had been added. His shoulders hunched; his gaze kept flicking between the empty chair and the entrance. He nudged the spare cup a finger's width, then squared the utensils beside it, preparing for a guest he wasn't sure would sit.

Two boys who had once shared everything. Now the domes themselves enforced the split: Eulər with his lectures on epigenetic science, Casper in his hall of mystic practice and spirituality. Different schools. Different worlds. Each tugging them farther apart.

Movement at the door pulled Casper's focus hard. Eulər.

He entered with a gait that wasn't quite his own—slower, shoulders bowed under some unseen weight. Casper's chest tightened. He knew that walk. Something was wrong. His breath stalled mid-inhale. He set his cup down too hard, ceramic clicking against the table.

When Eulər's eyes lifted—taking in the room, then landing on him—heat flared through Casper's skin. He'd suspected it. *Now the certainty came sharp as a blade.*

Dr. Bozwell's voice faltered, sensing the static. The filtration vents filled the gap, a faint mechanical breath that seemed to sync with Casper's pulse.

Eulər didn't move closer. He stood at the edge of the table, eyes unfocused—as if he wasn't seeing in three dimensions but in probabilities. Casper caught it: the same cold precision Eulər used when dismantling neural code. Not anger. Measurement. The distance between their realities.

Casper's fingertips pressed into the tabletop as if testing its steadiness.

He forced a calm he didn't feel, smoothed the front of his jacket with a flat palm—abandoned the gesture halfway. "You're late," he said, and his voice cracked on the second word.

His fingers found the cup's rim again. Not to lift it. To hold it in place—steadying a thought before it escaped.

Eulər's voice cut straight through the motion.

"You accessed the archive without authorization."

Dr. Bozwell straightened, chair scraping lightly. "What archive?"

Neither answered him. The air seemed to fold inward around the two men, isolating them in the soft shimmer of the restaurant's light.

Casper leaned forward, the tremor in his hand selling him out. "I had to verify what you were hiding," he said. "The Gamma Field has changed since our last incursion. It's responding now."

Eulər's jaw tightened. "You broke the pact."

Casper didn't react at first. His breath clipped short, chest stuttering as if his body had forgotten the sequence. A thin pulse sparked behind his eyes—too fast, too bright—splintering his focus. When he finally caught air, it felt grainy in his throat.

He swallowed. "You don't understand. It's conscious, Eulər. It knows us. If we ignore it, it'll come through on its own terms."

A flicker—fear, or recognition—crossed Eulər's composure. *Then, barely audible: "Then it already has."*

Eulər's eyes stayed still, but his voice hardened. "It knows the pact. That's why it's coming back through us."

Casper flinched—not at the words, but at the certainty behind them.

"It doesn't want to erase us," Eulər said. "It wants the vow kept."

The look was the same as thirteen years ago, when they were thirteen. Eulər had taken him beyond their early attempts to expand consciousness, sat him cross-legged, whispered the way into stillness. Casper closed his eyes, obeyed—and when he opened them again, he was no longer only a boy in the dome but a witness to something vast.

The Gamma Field. His first transcendence.

The old fear pressed against the inside of Casper's skull, the way it used to just before the Field stripped their thoughts apart. *The memory didn't arrive gently. It seized him.* His grip tightened on the table. His pulse stuttered. The room narrowed, and the door to what he kept sealed swung open.

The room smelled faintly of solder and insulation—a boy's laboratory passed down from his father. Wires ran in careful braids along the wall, feeding a cluster of processors humming on low power. At the center, two headsets rested on a table: matte black, a thin line of gold circuitry that shimmered when touched.

"Here. Put this on and don't take it off until I tell you we're safe," Eulər said.

"Safe?" Casper let the word hang. "Safe from what—your calculation for specific mental alerts?" His mocking laugh died when he saw Eulər's eyes. "What is this headset for?"

"It harmonizes our brainwaves to the same frequency and binaural rhythms as the Gamma Field," Eulər said. He slid his own headset on, wire threading into the console. "Entry and exit. We won't make it out if we lose the rhythm, so leave it on—until I tell you it's safe."

Casper hesitated, then obeyed. The foam cups sealed over his ears. At first, nothing. Then—like the faint hum of an electric fence—he felt it. Resonance. Not heard, but known. A subtle oscillation between hemispheres, an interference pattern that raised his skin and thinned his breath.

His body dissolved into mirages of sensation. Limbs displaced, stretched, as if memory itself were reassigning their boundaries. Thought became an elusive fish, darting from his grasp.

"Executing the code in five seconds," Eulər said, fingers hovering over the holographic HUD. "The next thing you'll know is the complete emptiness of the Gamma Field."

"What do you mean, complete emptiness—?" But the countdown vanished into zero. The headset pulsed. The HUD flared. And consciousness folded inward.

Casper tried to gasp—no breath came. *They were outside themselves. A void stripped clean of tether. The absence hit first: not silence, but subtraction.* Hunger, thirst, longing—gone. Even the quiet itch of a body waiting to be scratched—gone. The machinery of want and relief had been cut away, leaving awareness without weight.

It should have been the Buddha's promise made manifest—except the thought wouldn't hold. Terror came first. Without craving, there was no compass. Without sorrow or joy, no contrast. Casper tried to name what he felt, and words crumbled as they formed.

A spike of panic followed: *Nirvana—if that word applied at all—offered no bliss, only the sense of being stripped past retrieval.*

Fear rifled through him like static through an unshielded wire. He reached for Eulər —at least the presence that was Eulər—and in that contact they both knew: they weren't prepared. The emptiness would erase them if they lingered.

"The code isn't working," Eulər said, voice fracturing, syllables thinning toward transparency. Even language was being erased. "Cannot control the HUD—"

Casper clawed for the console interface, but his commands met a barrier: ACCESS DENIED. The letters floated dim, then dissolved into unreadable glyphs. "We have to get out of this field!"

The pullback came brutal, like being yanked through the aperture of a collapsing star. The hum receded. Breath returned. Casper blinked—Eulər's pale face in the console glow. The headset tore free, foam dragging against his temples.

They sat in silence, two teenage boys with sweat pooling at their collars, ordinary gravity pinning them like an anchor. Only later would Casper find the words for it.

The Field had not been dual.

"Never again," Eulər whispered.

Casper nodded, throat too dry for speech. When he finally found words, they came as a vow: "We make a pact. Never again. We cannot use transcendental meditation to join the Gamma Field. It's too dangerous."

Eulər extended his hand. Casper clasped it—palms slick, grip iron.

"If we break it," Eulər said, "it will be the end of us."

The handshake lasted longer than boys their age should have held. They waited until the words sank into marrow, until camaraderie fused with fear. Only then did they let go.

The room paused with them. No vent-breath. No scrape of movement. Even the processors' hum dipped low, as if the dome itself were waiting for one of them to move first. Neither did.

They were inseparable once. The pact worked against them. Their differences came to light and drove them farther apart with every passing season.

Back in the restaurant, Casper's mouth moved before he realized he'd spoken.

"Empty... it was empty—" Casper whispered, eyes unfocused.

Chapter Six

The Vow Held the World Together

☐ Location: Industrial Dome 2, Restaurant

Time Remaining: 99H 21M 39S until the Gamma Field vanishes.

The Source Listens for: the softening of a heart once formed by division.

The chef emerged from the kitchen with the composure of a man who had once conducted flavors on a planetary scale. Once the Master Food Conductor for General Mills on The Mars Portal, he had orchestrated entire populations' appetites with a flick of his palate. Now, recruited by the Kuudere, he ran this restaurant as though it were another laboratory, with every plate a controlled experiment and every patron an unwitting subject.

He recognized Councilman Dr. Bozwell instantly. The chair of the Elders needed no introduction. For years he had wondered why Dr. Bozwell never crossed his threshold, whether some secret slight had barred him from the circle of men who mattered.

He placed his right hand over his abdomen and bowed, the gesture halfway between humility and accusation. A salute unrecognized by Kuudere.

"What a high honor to have you here in my restaurant," he said, his tone wrapped in silk but edged with iron. "Though it escapes me what I did to offend you. All these years and this being the first time for your visit."

His words carried more than courtesy. They carried resentment. The chef, a white man outspoken about the rights of white men, had long felt excluded from the currents of power he believed were his birthright. Today, seeing Dr. Bozwell seated with companions—Casper and Eular among them—he felt the collision of recognition and grievance, a stage finally set for his performance.

"There was never any offense," Dr. Bozwell was quick to reply. His tone was clipped, the voice of a man who lived in the tempo of duty. "There isn't an opportunity to enjoy leisure in my work on the council of Elders."

The chef didn't wait for the rest of Dr. Bozwell's words. He leaned in, his voice pitched to carry beyond courtesy.

"No, I suppose when you govern a planet of over fifty million Kuudere—of whom seventy-four percent are white, and half are men—you have no time for them. All the majority whom you ignore. Instead, you favor every minority fragment of anyone not white and not male. Why favor the minority?"

His eyes narrowed, as if he had been rehearsing this indictment for years, saving it for this first confrontation.

"Is that why you never come to my restaurant? Because it is majority-owned? If I were anything but a white man, you would have been here sooner. More frequent. More welcome."

The accusation hung between them, not just a challenge to Dr. Bozwell, but to the entire order the Elders claimed to represent.

"The council does not favor any segment of the population," Dr. Bozwell said. His voice carried the weary discipline of one who had spoken these denials a thousand times before. "Every one of the Kuudere adds to the spice of life."

"Spice!"

The word detonated out of him. He rose on his toes, a wide sweeping arc with hand and arm, heat following his movements. The air around the open kitchen shifted—seared butter, starch, something turning acrid. A few diners froze mid-bite; the room seemed to pulse once, then still.

He dragged a chair from a nearby table and spun it backward, straddling it like a stage pulpit.

"As head taste conductor at General Mills, I learned what spice truly is. Not culture—control."

He leaned forward, voice lowering into the kind of clarity that made men listen even when they hated themselves for it.

"You think you know flavor? Nobody does. Every chip, every cracker, every bar—engineered. Salt isn't salt, it's a switch for the sodium channel. Sugar doesn't soothe—it detonates. We lace it with ethyl maltol until it sings through the skull. MSG? That's not seasoning—it's a tuning fork for the brainstem. And fat—structured triglycerides woven with diacetyl—wraps the tongue, drags the flavor down your throat, and whispers for another bite."

He tapped two fingers on the chair back, each strike like a tick of the metronome running the world.

"That's the role of the taste conductor—not to feed, but to compel. To make consumption instinct. To make need sound like choice."

He paused. The only sound was the soft clatter of a fork set down somewhere across the room.

"You had me fired from my position on The Mars Portal for creating and using Flavor 37." He inhaled sharply. "Then made me the chef of Dome 3 restaurant. Yet, that's what your Elders do with politics. Flavor and fairness—both engineered. You've weaponized compassion the same way I weaponized hunger."

He leaned closer, the sharp scent of scorched oil following him.

"You make the tiny spices—the minorities—more powerful than the natural order. You ruin the dish."

Casper felt the cadence of the chef's rant shift—sharp, then unstable, like the resonance spikes he'd seen in the meditation logs before the anomalies began. The same distortion pattern. The same rise in signal when a mind lost its mask. For an instant the room vibrated at the edge of something uncontained, the way the Gamma Field pulsed before it took someone.

His wrath expanded. "Education. Labor. Lending. Wages. Every law a pinch too heavy, until the stew turns bitter. The majority be damned for being the majority."

His jaw flexed, breath tight.

"You call it justice. I call it punishment. Punishment for being white. For being men who won't kneel. We built this planet with our creative vision, our money and leadership—our blood—and now we're told to apologize for it."

A hush spread outward from the table like heat from a stove. Chairs eased back. No one met Councilman Dr. Bozwell's eyes.

"Enough," the chef said, voice measured now, not shouting—performing. "We, the white men who still remember what it means to protect our own, will not watch our lives reduced to garnish. Enough is enough."

Casper let the words settle. *Masking agents.* The phrase caught on something in him. The air felt thick, though nothing in the room had changed. His breath entered shallow, left uneven. The discipline he relied on did not fail—it simply did not arrive. The signals stayed where they were, loud, unresolved.

He had spent half his life teaching initiates to unmask—breath by breath, thought by thought—until the world's color stopped lying. In meditation, the rule was simple: every sense was a gate, not a truth. Taste, smell, touch, all of it only signals bouncing off mind. Let the mind watch, and the signal fades. Reality remains.

But here, in this place, the science had reversed that rule. They had used taste and smell to make illusion feel real. To soothe panic. To tell the body it was full when it was starving. He wondered if Dr. Bozwell ever saw the symmetry—his policies built the same dream the domes now preached: a perfect calm that required blindness to maintain.

He looked at his plate. The food smelled of nothing. A designed absence. The same quiet he found in meditation, but inverted.

The words lingered, heavy as smoke, and for a long moment the only movement in the room was the shimmer of the heat lamps, humming like a low mechanical pulse.

The chef's tirade left a silence as thick as broth. Dr. Bozwell sat straight, the lines of his suit precise, his expression carved from patience. A single bead of moisture slid from his temple to his jaw. He brushed it away, slow and deliberate, as if denying its existence might preserve authority. Beneath the table, his fingertips pressed the napkin's edge until the fabric cut faintly into his skin. His whole career had been built on the expectation that the title "Chair of the Elders" carried its own gravity. He believed men should lean forward when he spoke, not challenge him.

"There was never any offense," he repeated, slower now, each word polished like a bead of glass. "The council's work demands of me constant vigilance. There is little leisure for dining, however fine the establishment."

His tone rang with the cadence of official statements. It was the same voice he used before assemblies, before citizens, before grieving widows and triumphant victors alike. Smooth, symmetrical, and hollow. He had mastered the art of saying nothing while sounding inevitable.

The chef's lips curled. He smelled the emptiness in Dr. Bozwell's reply as keenly as garlic searing in a hot pan. He leaned forward again, straddling the chair with theatrical command, his arms draped across the backrest as though it were a lectern.

"Vigilance?" His laugh cut sharp. "You call it vigilance when seventy-four percent of your people—white, half of them men—stand ignored, invisible in your so-called harmony. You preach equality while baking division into every law you pass. Education. Labor. Housing. Lending. Wages. These limits designed to hobble men who built this planet with their minds and their blood."

He slapped the chair-back twice, in rhythm, like a drumbeat punctuating his sermon. Diners nearby shifted uneasily, but he fed on their discomfort, his voice swelling.

"You dress it as fairness, but it is punishment. Punishment for the crime of being white. Punishment for the crime of being men who refuse to kneel. And then you speak of spice, Chair Dr. Bozwell—as if your little metaphors could season away the rot you've sown. Spice!"

Dr. Bozwell did not flinch. He folded his hands, composed, his gaze steady as if listening to a petition from a restless citizen. His reply came with the same empty luster, voice deep and practiced, carefully stripped of any true defense.

"The council does not punish. The council unites. Every Kuudere, regardless of origin, regardless of form, adds to the fabric of life. It is not division—it is harmony."

Dr. Bozwell noted the rhythm of the man's accusations. He had heard versions of them before—race, men, punishment, imbalance. Always the same pattern. Always the same certainty. He let the words pass through him, waiting for the next escalation. He paused, expecting the words to land like scripture, expecting the dignity of his office to silence dissent. But the chef's eyes glittered with the pleasure of blood sport.

"Harmony?" the chef hissed. "You sound like an advertisement. Words without marrow. Do you even hear yourself?"

He stood, towering over the table now, his movements precise, theatrical. He spread his arms as though addressing not three men but an entire assembly hall.

"You call it harmony to strip power from the majority. You call it fairness when you tilt every law toward the sliver, the fraction, the minority. You weaken the natural order, seasoning the stew until the meat is drowned in garnish. That is not harmony. That is poison."

A pulse twitched at the base of Dr. Bozwell's throat—one beat, then another, harder. He felt that pinch in the throat where you can't swallow but you need to. His breath slipped out of rhythm, shoulders rising before he caught them and forced the air back into its practiced cadence. The control returned, but not cleanly; a hairline fracture remained in the symmetry he depended on.

Casper drew a slow breath, expecting the familiar descent into stillness. *It didn't come.* The air caught wrong in his chest, shallow, off-tempo. A faint tremor threaded through his jaw—small, but real. For the first time in years, the discipline didn't settle him. *The room's signal was too loud*. He waited for correction. None came.

Casper shifted in his chair, sensing the weight of the moment, but Dr. Bozwell remained unshaken. He adjusted his cuff, eyes fixed on the chef as if the man were a common agitator. A small tremor passed beneath his sternum—recognition, not sympathy. The chef's rant wasn't about food at all; it was about architecture, the same tuned signals the domes used to keep millions sedated under the promise of calm. For years he assumed Dr. Bozwell's rigidity came from conviction. Now he wondered if it came from fear—fear of losing control over the levers that shaped what people believed they were choosing.

"Your metaphors are colorful," Dr. Bozwell said smoothly, "but this council governs not by hunger, not by appetite. It governs by reason. And reason demands balance."

The words rang with polish, but offered nothing to bite. Dr. Bozwell thought that enough.

The chef leaned close, so near his breath touched Dr. Bozwell's cheek. "Reason?" His whisper cut sharper than his shout. "I was the conductor of appetites. I know what men crave, what they cannot resist, what drives them past reason. You lecture of balance, but I can bend the marrow of men with a gram of glutamate. You, Chair Dr. Bozwell—you only bend them with empty promises."

Then, as abrupt as a curtain falling, he straightened, smoothed his jacket, and lifted the chair into place. His smile returned, brittle with false courtesy.

"But for now," he said softly, "enjoy my restaurant."

The scent of overworked oil lingered now, clinging to the skin, to the cuffs of their sleeves. Casper felt it on his palms—a thin film of something that wouldn't wash away.

Chapter Seven

A Fracture in Friendship

☐ Location: Industrial Dome – Restaurant

Time Remaining: 98H 57M 04S until the Gamma Field vanishes.

The Source Listens for: the hesitation before choosing the self over the whole.

Dr. Bozwell let the chef's words hang a moment, then drew a deep breath, gaze steady, voice filling the space with a warmth that quieted the room. He raised a hand—The One-Body Sign. Once used by the Elders, it signified the unity of one ruling body's authority. Long outdated. Some Kuudere still clung to the old ways. No one present returned the salute.

"You mistake us, friend," he began, his tone not clipped now but expansive, carrying the resonance of a man accustomed to commanding assemblies. "You speak of spice as control, of chemistry as compulsion, and in this you are not wrong. The food industry, with its scientists and conductors such as yourself, has given this planet more than nourishment. It has given solace. It has given continuity. It has soothed the tired worker who comes home to a meal that tastes as good today as it did in his childhood. It has given the grieving widow comfort in the sweetness of bread.

"These are no small contributions. You and your colleagues have cradled the minds of millions with invisible hands."

Someone at a distant table adjusted their chair, the scrape quick and apologetic—a reminder the room still existed beyond this table. A server passed behind Dr. Bozwell, the soft clink of plates brushing the edge of silence before he continued.

His eyes softened, though the cadence sharpened.

"But do not believe the Elders work otherwise. What you do with compounds and extracts, we attempt with laws and governance. Where you tune the brain's hunger, we tune the currents of society. Where you lace sugar with maltol, we weave justice with patience. Where you create a craving for another bite, we create a longing for another day lived in peace. We aim for harmony—not through illusion, not through favoritism—but through balance. You call us blind, and perhaps we are nearsighted. But blindness is not betrayal. It is only the imperfection of men working in a world too vast for any single vision."

He adjusted the cuff of his sleeve, smoothing a crease that wasn't there. His eyes flicked once to the mirrored panel behind him, uncertain whether it reflected or recorded.

Casper's voice slipped in, calm but edged. "Maybe there's no difference. Between seasoning a meal and drafting a law. Both train the mind to crave what it's given, not what it wants."

Dr. Bozwell set his hand lightly on the table, his voice dropping lower—intimate now—meant as much for the chef as for Casper across from him.

"You are wrong when you say we poison the people. Your opinions are not misguided—they are narrow. And narrowness is a hazard of genius. You see too deeply into one domain, and it blinds you to the wider view. The Elders labor, as you labor, for the well-being of all. We are not enemies, conductor. We are fellow craftsmen, though our mediums differ."

The kitchen doors hissed open and shut twice as staff moved through, the rhythm of the place continuing beneath the table's gravity.

The chef turned his head as movement caught his eye at the entrance. A figure paused in the doorway.

"I must get back to the kitchen. I'm glad we spoke, and I hope you'll return soon. Good luck bringing these two men back together. Perhaps they, too, have been ignored by the council too long."

Eulər's eyes darted to Casper, a silent question he couldn't voice. The moment passed—unseen by everyone except Dr. Bozwell. A server refilled a neighboring table's water glasses, the quiet glug-glug underscoring the sudden tightness between the three men.

The chef gave a curt nod and retreated toward the kitchen, his white jacket flashing once before the doors swung shut behind him. The table was left in silence, three men orbiting one another with unspoken expectations. The air in the restaurant was too clean, the recycled dryness catching in the throat—like breathing discipline itself.

Something in Eulər's breathing stuttered, a held truth snagging before it reached air.

Dr. Bozwell broke it first, still taken aback by the chef's sudden retreat. His voice carried the weight of lingering bitterness. Intended for the chef, it cut sharp.

"You're late," he said. "You know I detest lateness. An explanation, Eulər. Now."

Eulər clasped his hands in his lap, thumb grinding against knuckle. Words gathered but refused shape. The argument with Casper was still fresh, but the argument over who broke the vow would have to wait.

His mouth opened slightly. *One sentence would do it.*

Casper watched him now. Dr. Bozwell's attention hadn't shifted, but it pressed closer all the same.

Eulər closed his mouth. He reached for the water glass instead, drank, and set it down with care.

A response formed and vanished before it reached his mouth. He had to look away to keep it from returning. He stared—no quick reply—at the glinting water in front of him, catching fragments of his reflection, bracing a stronghold behind a neutral mask.

"I—" He faltered. "The transport systems are always broken. There were... complications."

Dr. Bozwell's eyebrows rose, the faintest crease of disdain breaking his otherwise sculpted expression. "Complications? You sound like a bureaucrat hedging for time. Speak plainly."

Eulər tried again, searching for ground that wasn't treacherous. "The Gamma Field has reemerged," he said finally. His voice was steadier than he felt. "After more than a dozen years. Its patterns are detectable again—about one thousand light-years away. Exactly where it was on the last appearance."

Dr. Bozwell exhaled through his nose, the sound halfway between a sigh and a huff. He gestured with an open palm, as though inviting Eulər to continue, but the movement carried impatience. His hand curled into a fist—then, with visible effort, he forced it open again. He sat very still, as though bracing against a pressure only he could feel.

The laughter around them faded in Eulər's ears, replaced by the image of Memphis's still body waiting in his studio.

"What does that mean, precisely?" Dr. Bozwell asked. "Do not waste my time with half-sentences."

"The rhythms are unstable. Entry and exit points don't align with prior data." Eulər's gaze flicked to the table, then away, never settling. "It's not just a recurrence—it's... louder." He shook his head once. "No. Not louder..."

A fork slipped from a patron's hand somewhere behind them; it hit tile—sharp, metallic—a small shock through the room.

Then Eulər stopped speaking. His jaw locked, but the rest of him went unnervingly still—shoulders squared, breath held, gaze fixed on Casper. The room tightened around that silence.

Dr. Bozwell's hand struck the table, sharp against the polished surface. "Enough. You've given me fragments, not facts. If I wanted riddles, I would consult a mystic."

Casper flinched at the word, ready to stand—chair legs scraping half an inch across the floor before he caught himself. He straightened slowly, jaw tight, hands folding together as if restraint itself were an act of obedience.

"Silence." Dr. Bozwell's voice filled the room with authority, his gaze slicing toward his son. Casper recoiled but didn't retreat entirely, lips pressed tight in rebellion. A tray clattered lightly against the counter at the far end of the restaurant—the nervous handling of someone who felt the mood shift.

Dr. Bozwell's attention pressured Eulər. The weight of that stare was like standing in a tribunal. "This Gamma Field—call it anomaly, call it whatever suits your science—it is not a gift. It is an obstacle. Do you understand me? An obstacle. The last visit destabilized our Dome life-support. Fractured our understanding of the universe... laws of physics... and I will have you explain its presence with clarity. No evasions. No distractions."

The kitchen doors flapped open again, the scent of seared spice drifting into the air, but none of them turned. Hunger didn't stand a chance against that tension.

Chapter Eight

A Child Hears The Field Breathe

Location: Industrial Dome – Restaurant

Time Remaining: 98H 22M 29S until the Gamma Field vanishes.

The Source Listens for: the memory that belonging was the first condition of life.

The restaurant's glass façade opened onto the endless churn of the gaseous world surrounding the domes. Bands of cobalt and slate clouds spiraled through the atmosphere, thick enough to blur the outline of the three distant suns. Their light bled through the vapor as pale smudges, like ancient lanterns fading behind smoke. From far beneath, the mechanical groan of the great vents reached upward—steady exhalations as the extraction arrays drew in poison gases and funneled them through chrome arteries running to the factories on Level Three. Each cycle made the floor hum, the vibration climbing into the table legs; silverware trembled, almost polite, with each pulse.

The domes never truly saw night. Darkness here was an emulation, a rhythm Tathagata system imposed to keep the flesh obedient to memory.

It measured hormone drift, blood chemistry, and fatigue, dimming the spectrum in calculated descent until the colony dreamed.

The suns outside raged unbroken, but the world inside turned on schedule, a closed loop of managed sleep and controlled renewal.

To the residents, that dusk felt real. To Tathagata, it was merely maintenance.

Councilman Dr. Bozwell sat with practiced composure, his knife moving through a plate of seared kelp-fish, slicing with precision though his eyes rarely left Casper. He chewed deliberately, the posture of a man who wanted his silence mistaken for authority. Across from him, Eulər touched nothing. His hand hovered over the rim of his glass, his thoughts elsewhere—on Memphis, on equations that refused to balance—while his ears strained for every syllable his once-upon-a-time friend spoke.

Casper's voice filled the space, softer than the mechanical hum outside, but it cut through like incense in stale air. He did not eat. His untouched plate steamed before him, the aroma of spiced roots mixing with the sharper tang of ionized gas leaking faintly from the ventilation shaft above. He spoke as though the Field itself leaned in to listen.

"The Gamma Field is no accident of physics," Casper began, his gaze on the swirling gas beyond the glass.

Eulər's jaw tightened. Dr. Bozwell's tightened too, by a fraction. Dr. Bozwell kept his knife moving, but the rhythm lost its ease. Eulər drew in a controlled breath—the kind he used to steady a drifting calculation—and let it out through his nose, unbroken.

The vents wavered against the table legs, a faint shift Eulər felt through his palms. *Odd*. He kept still, forcing his attention back to Casper.

"It is not storm, nor wave, nor particle stream. It is the vast Buddha Field—an ocean of bodhicitta so deep that even suffering itself dissolves before its tide."

The lights above flickered once—harmless recalibration, probably—but the timing gave his words a haunting emphasis. Eulər glanced up, then lowered his gaze at once, unwilling to grant the moment acknowledgment. Casper caught the shift and continued with more certainty.

"To touch it is to enter the realm where duality ends. Where self and not-self vanish like smoke. This is not dream or trance, but the marrow of Nirvana, hidden inside the bones of the universe."

Eulər lowered his glass, condensation smearing his fingertips. Outside, the faint shadow of a harvesting drone slid through the atmosphere, siphon tubes plunging into the mist.

Dr. Bozwell's fork paused mid-air. For the first time since the meal began, he stopped chewing. *Pressure rose behind Eulər's eyes—one clean pulse—then he forced it flat.*

"The ancients whispered of such a realm," Casper continued, hands motionless on the table. "They called it the garden where Sarva Shura moves without shadow, where Avalokita bends close enough to hear the cries of worlds, where the silent Bodhisattva of the Empty Sky teaches with no words. In the Gamma Field, they do not exist as figures, but as presences. Currents in the formless. Each one a gate. Each one a trial."

Dr. Bozwell finally lifted his fork, eyes sharp with skepticism, still saying nothing. The only sound was the faint clink of glass as a serving drone passed behind them and set down a tray at the next table.

Casper's words came slower now, deliberate, like stones placed into water. A vibration moved through the floor, sharper than before. Dr. Bozwell shifted his chair a few centimeters—the scrape short, deliberate. Eulər's fingers tightened around the base of his glass.

"Bodhicitta is not kindness. It is not morality. It is the raw will to end suffering—everywhere, for all beings. That pulses inside the Field, and it waits." Dr. Bozwell's fork halted above his plate. The gesture was quiet, but deliberate—enough to draw a thin line of heat along Eulər's spine. "It does not offer itself to the unready. To step into it unprepared is to vanish, to dissolve into an endless horizon of silence." A faint pressure flickered behind Eulər's eyes. He blinked it away, anchoring his breath against the chair's steady frame. "But to enter with courage, with surrender, with emptiness in the heart—then one stands in the place where death itself has no meaning."

Dr. Bozwell leaned back, chair creaking faintly against the vent-hum. His plate was empty now, but he kept the fork in hand and tapped it once against the table—an unspoken demand for proof.

Casper didn't flinch. He looked into the blurred glow of the suns beyond the dome, their light distorted by the planet's storms. "You call it anomaly. Your son calls it collision. I tell you it is the last refuge—the timeless ground from which every star was born and into which every star will one day fall. A door without hinges. A god without name. The end of all suffering."

For a moment, no one spoke, and even the restaurant seemed to hush.

Eulər cleared his throat. He tipped the glass, poured the last of his lager into his mouth; carbonation burned as it slid down. He set it down with a hollow clink and shifted in his chair, eyes narrowing toward the blurred glow of the three suns.

"It's not Nirvana, not some Buddha Field, not a heavenly realm," he said flatly.

Pressure shifted in his inner ear—a quick distortion—then passed before he could brace. His fingers tightened once on the rim. He let the sensation dissolve and held his posture.

Eulər kept his gaze on the suns, but his breath shortened. *A thin pulse ticked along the inside of his left wrist, quick and irregular, as if his body had noticed something his mind refused to name.* He shifted his weight, grounding himself through the chair frame against his spine.

For a moment the room tilted a degree to the left. Eulər steadied his hand against the table edge until alignment returned. He kept his eyes on the atmosphere beyond the glass, refusing to admit the disruption.

Outside the dome, the blue storm field shifted. The usual mosaic of drifting shades drew tight, pulling into a single, uniform plane of color. It held—unnatural, breathless—as if shielding some intruder from entering.

Eulər registered the uniformity, its precision too exact to dismiss. He straightened, expression neutral, though the shift had reached him. Then the mass folded in on itself and spun, breaking back into its swirling pattern.

He didn't look at Casper. He didn't look at Dr. Bozwell. He focused on the quiet between them, drew his next breath with care, and prepared the words he knew would move the room. *Silence pressed against him—exact, deliberate—as the Field itself waited for his first syllable.*

Dr. Bozwell leaned forward, fork still in hand like a gavel. "Well, what the driscol is it then? These theatrical pauses have tried my patience since you were a child—though that's likely why you do it."

Eulər straightened, shoulders setting into precise alignment. The fork in Dr. Bozwell's hand became still: no tapping, no shift in grip.

Eulər let the silence settle one moment longer, as if weighing whether the question deserved an answer.

Casper let out a short breath—almost a laugh—and looked away from Dr. Bozwell as if dismissing the outburst. Eulər's shoulders dropped a millimeter, the smallest sign the old authority no longer held the same force.

Casper smirked, leaned back, and folded his arms across his chest. His voice dripped with irony. "Here we go. Here come the scientific facts and data."

Eulər turned his head just enough to meet Casper's eyes. The look was calm, steady, and entirely without agreement. Then he returned his attention to the storm.

"Precisely," Eulər said, unbothered by the jab. His gaze drifted past them, out into the heaving atmosphere. Below, one of the massive vents opened its maw, a silver gash in the clouds, drawing in streams of gas that shimmered with pale lightning. The low drone vibrated through the tableware, as if punctuating his words.

"There is nothing in physics that can account for the existence of these Gamma Fields," he continued. "Yet from time to time throughout the universe, they appear. They remain for an unpredictable span of years, then vanish without a trace. This one—the one nearest our planet—has been here before. When we were much younger. And since then, the Dome System Mainframe has monitored the universe for its reemergence."

The glassware trembled, subtle and out of sync with the usual rhythm. A serving drone paused mid-glide beside the next table, motors holding for a single quiet beat before resuming.

Dr. Bozwell's eyes fixed on Eulər, unblinking, as though the air itself had narrowed around the table. His tone cut like sharpened steel. "That is not the sanctioned use or purpose of the Tathagata systems."

A brief ringing rose in Eulər's left ear. He blinked once, cleared the distortion, and placed both hands flat on the table to anchor himself. Only then did he speak.

He let the admonishment hang in the air like the scent of roasted roots from a nearby table. Then he leaned closer, ignoring the weight in his father's voice.

"It is evidence of a multiverse," he said, measured, deliberate. "Two universes colliding at the edges of their physical laws. When one touches another, it tears open a wound. The Gamma Field is the scar. Two different dimensions, two irreconcilable sets of physics. The collision unleashes destructive forces that, for a moment, create something our instruments can only call existence."

He paused to let the words sink in. *Beyond the glass, the atmosphere rippled with a violent shudder as a jetstream snapped against itself.* The dim suns wavered toward evening, their light reduced to ghosts in the haze.

"But this is different," Eulər said, lowering his voice. "*This time, our systems detect more than energy. They detect presence.*"

A soft static tick came from the sensor strip along the ceiling—too small for most patrons to notice. Eulər's focus snapped to it. He masked the reaction by adjusting the angle of his glass, but the fine muscles along his forearm tightened. *The timing was too exact to ignore.* The hair along his forearm prickled under his sleeve.

"Not anomaly, not radiation, not storm. A consciousness. Higher than ours. Waiting. Watching."

Casper gave a slow, deliberate shake of his head, his voice almost a whisper, heavy with defiance. "And you think mathematics can cage that?"

Eulər swallowed once—the motion controlled, but visible. He steadied his breathing before he answered, unwilling to give Casper the satisfaction of seeing the strain.

A vent pulse pushed a low vibration through the floor, sharper than before, as though the dome's internal rhythm had slipped a fraction off its mark.

"You think collision explains presence?"

The silence at the table thickened, broken only by the quiet scrape of Dr. Bozwell's fork against porcelain as he pushed his empty plate aside, eyes moving between them like a judge weighing two irreconcilable witnesses.

Dr. Bozwell's gaze returned to Eulər with a new weight—the kind reserved for someone who had crossed a line without permission. Casper caught the look and understood, for the first time, that whatever Eulər had sensed tonight, he was no longer sharing it freely.

Something unspoken had changed among them.

Chapter Nine

A Question Too Heavy

☐ Location: Industrial Dome – Restaurant

Time Remaining: 98H 07M 54S until the Gamma Field vanishes.

The Source Listens for: the shift when rivalry dissolves into recognition.

The holographic menu on the tabletop flickered, throwing pale green light across their faces. The faint hum of the massive suction tubes outside gave the restaurant its usual heartbeat, but tonight the rhythm felt off. Laughter in fragments, glassware clinking, low conversations from other tables drifting through the air like distant currents. The soft scent of warm spice tea mixed with the faint tang of ionized chrome from the air tubes—normally soothing, now metallic.

"It's not destructive!" Casper's voice rose, sharp enough to pull glances from nearby tables. His fingers tightened around the stem of his luminescent drink, and the soft light in the glass trembled with his grip.

Dr. Bozwell raised both hands, palms out, as if pushing back a storm. "It most certainly is," he said, voice cool, threaded with iron. "It drains our universe the way a black hole devours matter."

"It brings an end to suffering," Casper shot back, leaning forward. "An end to grief, to the emptiness of the struggle. Absolute joy in its wake—"

He and Eulər spoke over one another now, two waves colliding. The noise rose like the low rumble before a lightning strike. The Kuudere around them stilled. A group at the far table stopped mid-bite, heads tilting in a single motion. Bright, unreadable eyes fixed on the three men, watching, listening. Even the service drones slowed their silent orbits, as if pulled into the tension.

"Enough!" Dr. Bozwell's voice cracked through the noise like a gunshot.

The hush that followed was absolute. Conversations at other tables died mid-sentence; someone's spoon clinked against a bowl and stayed there. The air itself seemed to pause.

The stillness held. No chair scraped. No breath carried. Even the light from the holographic menu felt suspended, waiting for someone to break it.

Dr. Bozwell leaned forward, his shadow cutting across the holographic menu. "This is not suitable for everyone to hear. I want this—this experience or experiment, whatever it is you two are doing—to stop before someone gets hurt, or worse. Today. Right now. Do you understand?"

The words landed like a seal closing on a vault. A low vibration tremored through the floor as the massive suction tubes outside shifted pressure. The spice tea turned too sweet; the chrome turned sharp.

Casper started to explain, voice soft but urgent. "My team can continue with some levels of safety. The protective protocols, the coding—"

Dr. Bozwell cut him off with a flick of his hand. "No. It ends now. Until I have a council resolution, neither of you conducts further research into the Gamma Field."

Dr. Bozwell's voice stayed low but carried, like a tremor before a quake. "The dome systems of all five of our great habitats are failing."

He let it hang a heartbeat, letting every ear in the restaurant register it. Outside the panoramic windows, the dim YlnMn glow of the planet's atmosphere wavered, as if to echo his warning.

"The heating and ventilation systems self-destruct in the most unpredictable ways. Transport failures, too. Now the dome protective layers are corroding faster than ever."

At the table, Eulər sat back, silent. Too silent. His eyes lowered, fixed on the glass before him but seeing nothing. The tabletop glow painted his face in alternating bands of green and blue, colors shifting like a tide. Inside, his thoughts clawed at each other. His thumb pressed once against the ridge of the glass. A faint tremor passed through his hand, then stilled.

The choice settled.

Memphis. Her still body in his meditation chamber. No decay, no vitals, but not gone. A state beyond life but not death. If Dr. Bozwell stopped them now, she was lost. Out there somewhere beyond the Newtonian veil—and only he knew the path. *His father's decree sounded like a stone door closing, locking her away.*

Under the table, Eulər's fingers curled into his palm.

The holographic microphone pulsed once, scanning for input, then dimmed. The whole restaurant seemed to lean toward him—the silent Kuudere, the slow drift of scent and sound, the low hum of the tubes—waiting to see what the brilliant, quiet son of Councilman Dr. Bozwell would do next.

His jaw clenched. He said nothing.

But his mind was already plotting how to pull Memphis back.

He barely heard the rest of his father's words. *Something in him had already crossed a line.* The debate no longer mattered; the decision had taken root beneath it. If the Field held even a fragment of Memphis's signal, he would find her. He would breach the council ban, rewrite the codes, reroute power—whatever it took.

The silence between them wasn't surrender.

As Dr. Bozwell spoke, the lighting panels above shifted almost imperceptibly, throwing long, sharp shadows across their table. A service drone froze mid-glide, its luminescent tray trembling in the air. Even the low hum of the massive suction tubes outside seemed to falter.

"I need our systems focused on survival inside the domes," Dr. Bozwell continued, tone tightening, "not burning resources from Tathagata to surveil the universe or writing survival code for a transcendental visit to a Gamma Field."

He leaned forward, green glow washing across his hands like swamp-light. The room's scent—warm spices from simmering tea, the faint metallic tang of the ducts—turned acrid. All around, Kuudere diners sat stiff-backed, eyes unblinking, their faces catching the holographic reflections like masks.

"You two," Dr. Bozwell said, eyes shifting between them. "My brightest minds—and still you turn the same force into opposite faiths. One calls it annihilation. The other, paradise." He exhaled once, controlled. "It ends now."

The words slammed down like a gavel. The holographic menus blinked and dimmed, as though the restaurant itself were holding its breath. In that moment, the divide between science and mysticism—between black hole and paradise—felt like a living thing crouched at their table.

Eulər didn't look at Dr. Bozwell. He didn't need to. *The decision had calcified the moment his father spoke.*

He turned to speak.

Determined.

"If I could promise to stop, I would," he said. "But you raised me to seek truth, not permission. *I won't let her go.*"

Chapter Ten

The Shape of Fear

Location: Industrial Dome – Restaurant
Time Remaining: 97H 43M 19S until the Gamma Field vanishes.
The Source Listens For: the echo of a vow meant for the many.

"The reason I was late," Eulər said, voice low, deliberate, "wasn't just the transport system failing between Dome 1 and 3."

Casper leaned forward. Dr. Bozwell's eyes narrowed.

"Earlier today," Eulər continued, "I used my new methods—my equipment—to enter the Gamma Field."

Dr. Bozwell's hand slammed flat against the table. "I don't care how ingenious your methods are, or what discoveries you claim. No more experiments. No more contact with that anomaly. Until the Council of Elders decides otherwise, it ends here."

Eulər didn't flinch. His gaze locked on Dr. Bozwell's with a weight that dragged the air into silence. "It's gone too far to stop, Dr. Bozwell."

Something in his eyes—dark, scorched with knowledge—tightened Dr. Bozwell's chest. For a moment, the whole planet seemed to tremble under Dr. Bozwell's breath. *His son had called him Dr. Bozwell only once before, and that was when Eulər's mother had been killed.*

"What has happened?"

"You went without me?" Casper's voice cracked, higher than he meant. He grabbed Eulər's wrist hard enough to whiten his knuckles. "You swore, Eulər. You swore a promise."

Eulər met his eyes and did not answer. *Between them the restaurant's vent hissed—a thin, steady breath that sounded too much like the Gamma Field itself waiting.*

"It wasn't a promise to each other," he said finally. "It was a promise to what we didn't understand."

Casper shook his head. "That doesn't change what we swore."

"It changes everything," Eulər said. "The Gamma Field hears vows. It remembers them longer than we do."

Eulər twisted free—sharp, violent. "Listen to me." His words cut through Casper's anger like a blade. "It's worse than a broken promise. Worse than a system collapse."

The pause stretched. His throat worked, his face taut with the effort of saying aloud the thing he'd carried back from the Field.

Eulər's mouth opened, then closed. His gaze flicked to Casper, then to Dr. Bozwell, as if he couldn't decide which man had the right to hear it first. The hesitation was small but visible—a fracture in his control.

Then the name—barely more than breath, yet it shattered the room.

"It's Memphis."

A single breath moved through the restaurant—chairs stilling, utensils pausing mid-air. Even the vents seemed to hesitate. The word hovered between them, too fragile to touch, too heavy to ignore.

It hung there, unbearable. Casper didn't move. Dr. Bozwell didn't breathe. *For one beat, none of them seemed fully inside their bodies.*

A metallic tang crept through the recycled air, sharp and sterile, like the machines that kept them alive. It cut through warmth and food and human breath, reminding them how little in this place was ever truly organic.

"Memphis?"

"We practiced the protocol for days," Eulər said, voice barely above a whisper, yet it cut through the restaurant like a blade through glass. "She was ready—my best student. She wrote parts of the transcendental code herself. And we—" He swallowed, throat working as if it hurt to form the words. "Yeah. We ran the program."

Casper's jaw tensed, his fingers flexing against the tabletop.

"But she..." Eulər's gaze drifted beyond the dome's walls, as if he could still see the afterimage of the Gamma Field flickering at the corners of his vision. "She was excited by the sensation of non-suffering. It's intoxicating—an absence of pain so complete it bends your mind. I tried everything to keep her anchored in the meditation, but she was slipping. Dissolving from my focus." His voice cracked. "I wrote code on the fly, tried every channel, every counter-pulse to bring her back with me. But—"

"Stop," Casper snapped. Raw. Sudden. "I don't need the procedure."

Eulər closed his eyes. "I lost her."

A tray clattered somewhere across the restaurant—too loud, too sharp—someone startled by nothing but the silence around them.

For a moment, no one breathed. The dome lights stuttered, a faint flicker that seemed to echo his words. Outside, clouds churned harder against the barrier, static discharging in pale blue arcs. The storm pressed close, as if listening—its pulse syncing to the tremor in Eulər's voice.

Eulər's hand trembled, as if still wired to the machine that had taken her.

"When she crossed the threshold, the feed went wild—frequencies blooming beyond the visible range. The data collapsed into a single tone, like the hum of a dying star. And then..." He swallowed. "Then it spoke. Not in language, but in pulse. I felt her heartbeat merge with the signal until I couldn't tell which rhythm was mine."

He pressed his palms together, eyes glassed with disbelief. "The Gamma Field didn't consume her. It synchronized. It knew her. It answered."

A line surfaced in his mind, fossilized since childhood, back when his mother had whispered the forbidden page's warning: The voice of the Gamma Field is not command. It is remembrance.

The Book of Maha had not described the Field directly—but it had known what would come after exile. It had warned of a time when memory would rise to challenge preservation.

And now it was happening.

Casper's vision swam, the edges of the world trembling as though gravity itself recoiled. Bitterness filled his mouth, chemical and dry, as if the air had turned to dust. It wasn't fear exactly—it was the taste of knowing too much, too fast. *The thought came unbidden: If it knew her, it knows me.* The fear wasn't that Memphis was gone, but that she was still there—somewhere inside that living geometry—listening.

Dr. Bozwell leaned back, his composure fracturing. "You're saying the anomaly recognized the consciousness?"

Eulər didn't answer at first. His jaw tightened; the muscle tremored once. The dome's hum filled the pause, low and even, like something waiting.

His reply was barely audible. *"No, Doctor. It remembered her."*

What followed wasn't absence. It was awareness—settling over them like a held breath that would never exhale.

Casper surged forward, his chair screeching across the polished floor. "You lost my sister in the Gamma Field!" His voice ricocheted off the high dome ceiling, drawing the attention of nearby diners. "How is that even possible?"

Dr. Bozwell's hands hovered above the table, fingers trembling, but his tone stayed controlled—each syllable measured like a judge pronouncing sentence. "What do you mean, you lost her?"

"It's not a door," Eulər said, desperate now, "not a tunnel or a ship you step into. It's a protocol—mindful, yes, but not just thought. It's meditation driven by code. It's... both. The mind and the body begin to blur, to become a third level of consciousness. A place between."

Casper's fists trembled. "You're saying she didn't go physically, but she's still gone?"

"Yes," Eulər said. "When you transcend at that depth, there's no border between where the meditation ends and the Field begins. You go where it leads. We both did."

His knuckles were white, his face ashen. "But she... she didn't come back."

Dr. Bozwell looked from one to the other, his face carved with disbelief, fear creeping like frost at the edges.

Casper's voice, when it came, was no longer a shout but a raw, jagged whisper. "What do you mean you lost her—she's gone?"

The question hung in the dome like a suspended blade—no answer possible that would not cut. The silence after it felt heavier than gravity itself.

Chapter Eleven

We Break When We Reach Alone

▫ Location: Industrial Dome – Restaurant → Transit Hub

Time Remaining: 82H 18M 44S until the Gamma Field vanishes.

The Source Listens for: the thought untainted by desire to control what was once whole.

Dr. Bozwell's voice cut through the tension with deliberate calm, but his eyes betrayed something sharper—a father, not a scientist, demanding clarity.

"She is in the medical facility, with Dr. Gatlia?" His gaze pinned Eulər like a blade.

Eulər shook his head slowly, almost guiltily. "Not in the hospital. No... not with Dr. Gatlia either."

The words landed like stones. Casper leaned forward, knuckles whitening against the table. "Then where?" His voice cracked under the weight of dread. "Where is my sister right now?"

"In my meditation studio," Eulər admitted, the syllables grinding out as if they scraped his throat.

Dr. Bozwell blinked hard. "Your studio?" He leaned back, incredulous—then forward again, anger controlled but rising. "I thought you said she was lost."

"I did," Eulər said, pushing to his feet. He planted his palms on the table's cold surface, shoulders trembling under the weight of explanation.

"She is lost. Her body is here, but her state—her being—" He broke off, reaching for words that refused him. "It's like limbo. Suspended between here and…" His voice failed into silence.

He didn't mean to think of it, but the words from the missing page returned—The Book of Maha burning in his memory, more insistent now: "*There is no afterlife. There is only memory, waiting for permission.*"

He had once dismissed it as mystic poetry. Now it felt cruelly exact. Memphis wasn't gone. She was held—caught in the memory of a world that refused to release her.

"Limbo?" Dr. Bozwell's tone hardened to iron. "This is entirely reckless."

Casper shot upright, the air around him charged with rage. "Reckless? It's monstrous!" His chair clattered behind him as he jabbed a finger at Eulər. "You're telling me she's alive, but not alive—that she's trapped in some state you can't even name?" His voice broke into a shout that turned every eye in the restaurant toward them.

"Enough," Dr. Bozwell said, firm—though his hand trembled on the table edge. "We will not waste another heartbeat arguing in riddles." He rose to his full height, his right arm sweeping toward the exit, presence snapping the room into order. "We go there. Now. Together. I will see her myself."

For a moment, no one breathed. Then, in single file, they moved. The restaurant doors hissed open and released them into the bright corridor beyond. Diners whispered as they passed, hushed voices following like shadows.

The corridor lights shifted from white to amber. A soft chime rolled through the dome, too calm for what it meant.

ALL TRANSIT GATES TEMPORARILY HELD — STRUCTURAL STABILIZATION IN PROGRESS.

Casper felt the words land like a hand on his chest. Not now.

As they neared the transportation center, Dr. Bozwell slowed—then stopped. His eyes drifted upward, caught by the sheer enormity of the dome above. The translucent arc rose two miles overhead, a cathedral of glass and alloy, its surface faintly shimmering where protective fields faltered. The air tasted metallic here, sharp with ozone and the faint sting of acid carried in from the locks. He lifted his hand, finger trembling as he pointed.

"This," Dr. Bozwell said, motioning to the failing dome overhead, "has consumed every breath of my life. Keeping these structures alive so our people survive the storms—this is what Tathagata was built for, not scanning the void for whatever broke us in the first place. Until now, nothing was more urgent than this work."

He turned toward the transport gates, voice low, stripped raw. "But Casper's sister—what you've brought into this dome. If I'm abandoning it, then we're dealing with something greater than acid and entropy."

"The crews can't keep pace," he said. The crack in his usually stoic cadence made both Casper and Eulər turn fully toward him. "The erosion of the dome's protective shield is accelerating—faster than we've ever seen. If the acids chew through, even for a moment..." His words withered, leaving only the vast hush of the transportation plaza.

Beneath their boots, the tiled floor hummed with the vibration of the stabilizers. High above, scaffolds clung like fragile bones to the dome's curvature. Workers in exo-rigs hunched over panels that glowed with a molten sheen. Sparks cascaded down in glimmering arcs, raining light across the translucent sky.

Dr. Bozwell exhaled hard. "They've turned to a new liquid metal. The engineers believe it will withstand the acid storms better than the old composites."

The scaffold swayed in the distance, a dangling silhouette against the half-lit heavens. To Dr. Bozwell, it was a frail skeleton against the sky; to Casper, it was absurd anyone thought men could weld eternity shut; to Eulər, it was proof that entropy laughed at science.

And to Eulər, something older stirred beneath the weld-fire and scaffolds—something his mother once called the original grief. The Source had whispered it long before exile, long before systems. The line returned, crystalline and cruel: *"All structure is grief formalized. All grief is a structure waiting to fall."*

He hadn't understood it as a child. Now, watching the dome's skin flake and hum under pressure, he felt the truth of it like weight in his bones. *The dome wasn't just breaking. It was mourning.*

Eulər didn't look up at the cracks or the shimmer of stressed alloy. His attention stayed fixed on his father, steady and unblinking.

"It has always been urgent," he said quietly. "Since the dawn of conscious life, it has always been the same—struggle, patched by more struggle. Food, shelter, air. A body trapped by sight and sound and taste and touch. Every age calls it survival. But survival is just suffering with a name."

Dr. Bozwell turned toward him, anger rising—but Eulər didn't give him room to speak.

"What I use Tathagata for is not to extend the struggle. Not to weld a few more years onto a dying skin. I use it to replace the need for struggle at all. To liberate the Kuudere from everything that binds them to suffering. Once and for all."

The words weren't arrogant. They weren't a defense. They were fact—clean and final as the hum of the dome above them.

Casper froze between them, hearing not an argument, but two worlds pulling apart.

A repair cycle started somewhere high above—nothing urgent, just the routine creak of stressed joints settling as welders shifted their weight. The sound barely registered to the workers in the plaza; upkeep was as ordinary as the dome's artificial daylight. *A low shiver ran through the inner membrane, subtle enough to miss unless you were already afraid.* All three men felt it—an instinctive tightening, the kind the body registers before the mind can name it.

Then the maintenance voices drifted down, carried perfectly by the dome's hollow resonance.

"Boss, boss, I got it! Just crank the feeder to max and slap this goo on fast like frosting. We'll be back in the cafeteria before the soup goes cold."

Laughter echoed down the dome. Casper flinched before he could stop himself. The sound scraped against him—too light, too careless—like joking outside a closed medical door. Men could laugh about seams while his sister lay unresponsive in Eulər's studio.

But the tightness in his chest wasn't love. It was sour memory—the kind that sticks because it never resolves. He and Memphis had never been close; their childhood was marked by quiet hostility, a mutual awareness that they irritated each other simply by existing. She had chosen Eulər's transcendence work only to spite him, not because she believed. Casper had known it the moment she told him—tone sharp with the satisfaction of choosing the one path that would cut him deepest. She followed Eulər to wound Casper, not to honor the research. And Eulər—brilliant and blind—had never seen it.

A burst of static hissed across their comms as an older man sighed. "Reut, if you frost a cake too fast, it collapses into a puddle. Same with domes. You want to kill us with pastry metaphors?"

Reut laughed nervously, his exo-rig clanking against the scaffold. "You always talk food when we're fixing the sky. Last week it was cake, this week soup. You hungry, old man?"

"Always hungry," the maintenance Chief said, calm as a monk. "Hungry for patience. Hungry for wisdom. Hungry for not falling two miles through acid winds because some fool slathers metal like butter on burnt toast."

A spark shower rained down as the boy jammed the feeder too hard, his rig jerking sideways. The vibration reached the plaza floor, a faint shudder under Dr. Bozwell's boots. Eulər tracked the weld rhythm without meaning to. Six seconds on. Three seconds off. *He counted two full cycles before he realized what he was doing—and couldn't stop.*

"See? Seam sealed! Told you I'm a natural!"

For the briefest instant, the dome's field flickered—not enough for panic, just a thin stutter of light, almost like acknowledgment. Reut paused mid-motion, visor tilting. "Chief... did you hear that? The resonance is off again."

The gate display pulsed once, then refreshed.
NEXT DEPARTURE WINDOW: 00:01:48

Dr. Bozwell's thumb hovered over the priority channel. He lowered his hand instead. Even he couldn't order metal to cool faster.

Casper's throat tightened; the flicker pulled up Memphis's eyes the moment she slipped away. Eulər measured the stutter like he was measuring the limits of his own guilt. Dr. Bozwell set his jaw, the sound of failing fields as familiar to him as a heartbeat skipping under a monitor. Wanting desperately to be free of the crew and their chatter, he quickened their pace toward the transports.

"Natural fool," the Chief muttered, grabbing Reut's rig with the steady grace of someone who'd saved a dozen apprentices from killing themselves. "Let me tell you a story. Long ago, there was a farmer with a broken fence. He patched it with haste—hammer, no thought. That night, the wolf slipped through and ate his goats. He blamed the wolf. He blamed the wood. He never blamed the fool with the hammer."

"So what—I'm the farmer?"

"No. You're the goat."

Reut huffed, but his eyes flicked to a seam above them, narrowing. "The resonance is off today," he muttered. "You hear that?"

A beat passed. Then, high above, a seam groaned—not the usual settling creak, but a drawn metallic strain. Pressure building where it shouldn't. The laughter thinned, then stalled.

Reut went still in his rig. The Chief looked up, torch paused, head cocked.

"That's not us," he said.

The moment held—then slipped away before either man could name what had changed. The crew shook it off. Laughter rose again, louder, as if volume could drown instinct. The Chief returned to his weld with slow precision, liquid metal flowing like silver veins across the dome. The smell of scorched alloy drifted downward, acrid and sharp.

"You see, Reut," the Chief said, "the dome is no cake, no fence, no toy. It is skin—our skin. You rush it, you scar it. You scar it, you kill it. And then it kills us back."

"Fine," Reut huffed. "Slow and steady. Like soup simmering, right?"

"Exactly," the Chief said, the hiss of his torch steady, almost soothing. "Now—hand me the ladle."

"You mean the feeder gun?"

"Yes. The ladle of the sky."

Casper's jaw locked. Men could joke about seams and soup while his sister lay unresponsive, her body waiting for systems to decide if they were finished with her.

A sharp clang rang from another scaffold—metal striking metal too hard, too fast—followed by a brief warning chirp from the dome's monitoring array. The plaza below tightened around the sound.

Dr. Bozwell's hand dropped to his side. He cut the channel piping the crew's chatter into the plaza. His face stayed taut with grief, though his lips twitched despite himself. Casper exhaled through his nose, torn between rage at Eulər and a reluctant, ugly laugh at the exchange above. Even Eulər—ever-serious—allowed himself a small shake of the head.

He lingered a heartbeat, eyes following Reut's jerky movements. Something in the boy's urgency struck him—not talent, not skill, but rawness he had seen only in people the world wasn't done with yet.

Above them, Reut's laughter carried once more across the dome—thin, uncertain—then vanished into the structure he was trying to mend.

Dr. Bozwell finally turned toward the portal. His voice came low, grave again, weighted by more than atmosphere. "They joke because the alternative is terror. Remember that."

By the time the gate lights shifted back to white, none of them stood the way they had when they arrived.

Casper closed the distance between them faster than he meant to, driven less by the world around him than by the thought of Memphis waiting in that studio. A hollow drop opened in his chest—the kind that came before collapse. *For a split second he saw Memphis the last time she spoke: voice faint, eyes already drifting.* The image hit like a hand around his ribs. The dome's flicker matched his pulse—too fast, too thin—as if time itself were urging him forward.

Eulər followed with a stiff, braced posture, as if each step pressed harder on whatever explanation he still owed.

In silence, they moved into the transport center.

A tremor ran through the floor—the kind that didn't belong to stabilizers. All three paused, instinct lifting their chins as if the dome itself had briefly held its breath.

The doors slid apart with a sigh, releasing a gust of air cooler than the corridor, tinged with oil and the sterile bite of recycled oxygen. The platform lurched as the lock disengaged. Casper didn't exhale—not until the carriage sealed and the dome's laughter fell behind them.

The soundscape shifted immediately: gone was the hollow resonance of the dome, replaced by turbines, the layered thrum of magnetic rails, the faint mechanical chatter of gates opening and closing in rhythm.

The transport hub stretched cavernous before them, a labyrinth of platforms and corridors lit by strips of white light that stuttered every few seconds, as though exhausted by their own duty. The illumination gave the space an underwater quality, shadows swimming across faces and walls as crowds surged past.

Casper flinched at a sudden hiss—compressed gas venting somewhere behind the gates—and his pulse leapt to his throat as if the dome above had split open. He glanced up, instinctive, but found only steel rafters and the scuttling silhouettes of maintenance drones. His breath escaped sharp, embarrassed. He said nothing.

For a brief moment, as the hub lights stuttered overhead, he remembered the way Memphis had looked when she agreed to join his work—calm, intent, as though she finally saw the world the way he did. The memory steadied him. Whatever state she was trapped in now, she hadn't stepped toward the Gamma Field out of rebellion or panic.

Eulər walked with stiff precision, eyes cataloguing every sound, every flicker, the exact interval between the rail's magnetic surges. His mind, trained to see systems, found no comfort in patterns; their inconsistencies gnawed. Each tremor in the floor was a reminder of entropy, as undeniable as Memphis's still form waiting in his studio.

Dr. Bozwell carried the weight differently. His eyes didn't scan or measure. They absorbed. He moved with the quiet dignity of someone whose every step was a statement: I see what fails, I carry it, but I will not falter. Still, when the next overhead light buzzed, sputtered, and returned to dim life, the faint twitch in his jaw betrayed him.

The crowd pressed tighter as they neared the gates. Conversations clattered in overlapping tongues—urgent, distracted—each threaded with the same underlying note of unease. Bodies craned upward without realizing it, as though every Kuudere had learned the habit of doubt.

Casper leaned close to Eulər, voice low, dangerous. "When we reach your studio... if she's gone—" He stopped, words clawing at his throat. His eyes shone with fury that was half-grief, half-promise.

Eulər didn't meet his gaze. His voice went quieter still, nearly drowned by the roar of a departing tram. "She is not gone. Not yet."

Casper hesitated on the threshold, the rail's hum rising like a held breath. *His reflection shivered across the metal—one self solid, one ghosted by the stuttering light.* He stepped toward the carriage, then stopped. His body moved as if it remembered something his mind refused to face. *For an instant he couldn't breathe.*

"If she can hear us," he said, barely audible, "what will she know of what we've become?"

Eulər's answer came slow, stripped of certainty. "Only what remains when belief and proof collapse into the same thing." He stepped aboard first, as if moving toward judgment.

Dr. Bozwell's gaze followed them both. For all his authority, he looked older now, as though the dome's failing light had found the cracks beneath his composure.

"Then let this journey end with truth," he murmured, "not comfort."

They stepped onto the platform together. For a heartbeat, the entire hub seemed to pause: the air pressed heavy, the lights stuttered again, and the silence between them was more violent than any outburst.

The hiss of the doors sealing shut broke it.

And then, with a deep-bellied roar, the transport pulled them forward—into the dark channel that would carry them toward the meditation studio, and toward whatever waited there.

Chapter Twelve

The Moment I Doubt

☐ Location: Dome 1— Meditation Chamber A7 (Lower Stratum)

Time Remaining: 76H 54M 09S until the Gamma Field vanishes.

The Source Listens for: the shared pain that becomes a bridge instead of a wall.

Inside the meditation chamber, the air was colder than the rest of the dome—a sterile chill that gnawed through robes and skin. The walls were padded with sound-dampening fabric, white and seamless, making the chamber feel like silence hollowed out and furnished.

Dr. Gatlia worked on her knees at the center of the room, bent over the body, hands a blur of precision. Electrodes clung to Memphis's temples, throat, chest, and fingertips. Leads snaked into the monitor array beside her, and every line glowed, flatlined—no electrical spikes, no rhythm of life. Dr. Gatlia's lips moved in a hushed plea she didn't mean for anyone to hear.

"*Not another one,*" she whispered, breath sharp with exasperation. Two more probes. Three. A fourth check. The monitors hissed their refusal. Still nothing.

The door sealed shut behind the men with a pneumatic hiss. She hadn't heard them enter.

"What did you mean when you said, 'not another one'?" Dr. Bozwell's voice broke the chamber like a crack in glass—low, deliberate, impossible to ignore.

Dr. Gatlia jolted, caught in her own words. Her gaze darted to Casper first, then to Dr. Bozwell. Shame flickered across her face. She rose, dusting her knees with trembling fingers, and held the One-Body Sign: palm up, open hand, horizontal across the sternum. A ritual greeting no one demanded anymore.

"Thank you," Dr. Bozwell said, acknowledging it with the weight of an elder. His voice softened, almost kind, though his eyes did not blink. "You know that tradition is no longer a requirement."

"Not a requirement," Dr. Gatlia said, steadying herself. "But still a right."

Her tone sharpened as she faced the reality before them. "Memphis shows no sign of life. Her brain and organs respond negatively to stimuli. By every known definition, Memphis is dead."

The words landed like lead. For a moment, none of them spoke.

Then the air shifted—soft, almost sweet. Not floral, not chemical. Something beyond recognition. It moved through the chamber like memory from another world. Dr. Bozwell's breath caught; Dr. Gatlia turned her head slightly, searching for its source.

Casper inhaled, then broke the silence. "Do you smell that?" he whispered. "It's like…" He stopped, unable to name it.

Dr. Gatlia's eyes watered, though she didn't cry. "It's not decomposition," she said, voice unsteady. "It's something else."

Eulər's voice came from behind them, low—almost reverent.

"Odor sanctitatis. The odor of sanctity," he said. "The ancient theologians wrote that the dead who were truly awake released it—not rot, but release itself."

The scent drew them closer in spite of themselves. It wasn't perfume or incense, or anything cataloged in the Kuudere archives. It had no analog, yet it felt intimate, as if the body itself exhaled serenity. It made the sterile cold seem almost merciful.

Dr. Bozwell's chest tightened. The sweetness clung to thought, inviting surrender. *For an instant he felt the absurd wish to kneel beside the body—not in mourning, but devotion.* His voice came pained and accusing.

"This doesn't look like liberation from suffering."

Eulər's head twisted slightly, a controlled snap of disbelief. Dr. Bozwell's dismissal wasn't new—just another fracture laid atop the others from the restaurant, the council, the lab, his childhood. But the weight of them landed now, in this room, at this body.

His gaze drifted back to Memphis. Something had changed since he left her. Her skin—he blinked hard—was faintly translucent. Not glossy. Not pale. Translucent. Along the cheekbones, the line of her neck, as if the tissue itself had thinned by degrees.

Recognition tightened his spine. *The Field is learning.*

Learning how to take the consciousness and the body.

Soon it would understand how to take the whole being.

His jaw worked once before he stilled it, restraint colder than the room. The next break, he knew, would not be his.

Casper stumbled forward, dropping to his knees beside his sister. He took her hand as if to warm it, thumb tracing the unyielding cold of her knuckles.

"She can't be dead," he murmured—then louder, as if volume could force reality to comply. "She can't be dead."

His voice cracked but refused to break. He folded her fingers into his palm, flexed her arm at the joint. No stiffness. He lifted her wrist and bent it gently.

"Look," he whispered, eyes wide with the desperate logic of a drowning man. He paused, breath shaking, as if waiting for her to inhale on her own. "There is no decay. No rigor mortis. If she was dead, we would see it."

Casper lifted her hand and pressed it to his throat, as if asking her pulse to remember his.

"You don't get to leave like this," he said quietly. It wasn't a plea. It was a rule he had lived by. Her skin was already cooling, but he held it there longer than necessary, longer than polite.

Gatlia looked away first. Something intimate had happened in the room, and none of them consented to it. He looked up, meeting Dr. Bozwell's stare with fevered intensity.

"See? She's not dead."

Dr. Gatlia exhaled sharply, as though testing the air itself. "Strange," she murmured, pressing her tongue to the roof of her mouth. "No taste. Not metallic, not sterile—nothing." She paused, unnerved by her own words. "It's as if the gustatory response has been nullified. I can't register flavor or texture." Her tone faltered. "That shouldn't be possible."

Dr. Bozwell glanced at her, unsettled by the clinical phrasing—because behind it he heard fear.

He stood rooted, caught between reason and something far more dangerous: hope. His gaze flicked over Memphis's still form, the monitors' dead readouts, the hush of the chamber. And inside his mind, the storm broke loose.

Cold settled at the back of his throat. His pulse slowed, not from calm but refusal. He waited for someone else to speak. No one did.

They told me at the restaurant.

Euler with his cold science, Casper with his burning mysticism. Two men arguing over the same abyss.

The Gamma Field.

Casper calls it a Buddha Field—a heaven without suffering, the end of duality. A paradise. Euler insists it's the clash of universes, a multiverse rupture, physics tearing against itself. Both of them said the same thing without knowing it: it is not natural. It does not belong here. No law of probability should have birthed it.

And yet it has—twice. Once, twelve years ago. And now again, closer. Hungrier.

Meanwhile the domes are rotting. Every system crumbles faster—air, water, food. Viruses whisper through the vents like assassins. We are a civilization counting the hours of our breath, and these two men spend their brilliance not on survival but on courting this anomaly, this... Field.

And Memphis.

She was their experiment, their volunteer, their sacrificial lamb—trained for transcendence, pushed through their protocol. And now she lies here: body intact, soul exiled. Dead by every instrument, yet not dead enough for nature to claim her.

What did Dr. Gatlia mean—not another one? How many others went into this so-called meditation and came back as husks? Why didn't they tell me?

And why does Casper look at her body as if he knows something I don't? His insistence isn't just grief—it's certainty. He's seen a sign. Or worse: he's hiding knowledge.

The chamber pressed in on him, soundless except for Casper's trembling breaths. Dr. Bozwell's fists tightened at his sides. The pieces clattered in his mind, refusing to lock into place. Dr. Gatlia's slip, Eulər's evasion, Casper's stubborn faith—it all stank of omission.

Dr. Bozwell seized on the only thought that still obeyed him.

This is a procedural failure.

Instruments fail. Systems drift. Calibration lags under stress. That wasn't philosophy. That was maintenance.

He repeated it silently. *Maintenance.*

The word felt thinner the second time.

The chamber did not respond to it. Neither did the body.

He anchored himself there, gripping the idea like a rail in turbulence. Not transcendence. Not memory. Not reunion. Just a flaw moving faster than protocol could name it.

Something is missing here. Something vast.

His gaze drifted to the faint hum of the electrodes, their light too steady, too knowing. A phrase from Casper's earlier arguments returned—language shapes perception; perception collapses reality. He had dismissed it as mystical jargon. Now, staring at Memphis' unmoving chest, he felt the words in his mind shift, rearranging themselves until they formed a hypothesis he did not want to test. *If thought can change the Field,* he realized, *then the Field can change thought.*

For a breath, the chamber dissolved. He was back in Dome 1's observatory twelve years earlier, with Eulər's voice echoing off the glass, quiet and certain. "The Gamma Field isn't destruction, Dad. It's release. When resistance ends, there is no death—only translation." Dr. Bozwell had laughed then, that tight, polite laugh of disbelief. It was inspired and cute coming from a twelve-year-old.

But now, with Memphis lying between breath and stillness, the phrase took root in him like infection. *Release.* What if this was what liberation looked like—order dissolving into perfect coherence?

Dr. Bozwell stepped closer to the body, his voice calm but edged with iron. "Then tell me," he said, eyes locking first on Dr. Gatlia, then on Casper. "If she is dead, why does she not decay?"

No one answered.

Dr. Gatlia reached for the console—then stopped.

Her fingers hovered a breath away from the glass, close enough for the light to pale her skin. The array responded anyway, dimming half a shade, as if acknowledging intent without contact.

She withdrew her hand slowly. Said nothing.

Dr. Gatlia turned back toward the array, fingers hovering inches from the switches.

"Because she's still resonant," she said finally, voice low, almost reverent. "Her cells are still tuned to the Gamma frequency."

Dr. Bozwell's brow furrowed, calculation forming.

Casper rose halfway, eyes gleaming with the fever of belief. "You see? She crossed and hasn't come back yet. The Field holds her between."

The air thickened. The monitors flickered once—one pulse, then gone. Dr. Bozwell checked the timecode again. Three days, counting backward. The display held steady, as if mocking expiration.

Eular stepped forward and reached behind the monitor stack. He didn't look at the display as he powered one unit down. Not all of them. Just one. The room did not grow quieter, but the silence settled differently, redistributed.

He stepped back into place. He did not comment on what he had changed.

Dr. Bozwell leaned closer until his breath fogged the glass.

"System lag," he muttered, too fast.

No one answered.

Then a single eyelash lifted from her cheek and floated upward—against gravity.

Dr. Bozwell stepped back, every instinct torn between awe and dread. "Between what?" he demanded.

Dr. Gatlia's eyes met his.

"Between existence and its reflection."

The monitors flickered once more—one pulse, then gone. The air changed again. Slightly colder. That same scent—soft, nameless, luminous—rose faintly from nowhere and everywhere at once. *It wasn't just from Memphis now.* It came from the walls, the breath, the thought. Dr. Bozwell's mind wavered between awe and terror. The odor carried a gravity that seemed to pull the chamber inward, as if *the Gamma Field itself were breathing through them*, testing their willingness to be dissolved.

Dr. Bozwell understood then—not as insight, but as threat—that the Field was no longer observing them.

It was waiting to see who would step forward first.

Chapter Thirteen

The Field Looks Back

Location: Dome 1— Meditation Chamber A7 (Lower Stratum)

Time Remaining: 71H 29M 34S until the Gamma Field vanishes.

The Source Listens for: the surrender of pride that once kept unity apart.

Eulər's voice cut through the hush. "It's a code that protects us when we transcend the natural body." His hands moved as he spoke, drawing invisible diagrams in the air.

"Consciousness leaves and travels where the Self directs it. But the code keeps the physical and the consciousness tied. There is something there—the Gamma Field. It wants the consciousness. *If it breaks the code...*" He hesitated, throat dry. "I assume consciousness leaves, but the body remains."

Eulər's fingers twitched toward the console beside him, pulling up a floating schematic—thin white lattices pulsing with ghostlight.

"We mapped the exodus pattern across seven neural matrices," he said, voice low but charged. "Each time consciousness begins to phase, the bioelectric envelope fractures in microsecond increments—thirteen frames before total dissociation. The body remains alive, but blind. The code intercepts that fracture, folds the quantum residue back into the soma, forces a loop."

His hand passed through the projection, distorting the data as if even the light resisted the truth.

"*It's not perfect*. The code strains every time it's invoked, like a muscle tearing under its own command."

Dr. Gatlia's calm broke for a moment. She leaned forward, eyes flashing.

"And what happens if the loop doesn't close?"

Her voice carried a note that wasn't curiosity. It was memory.

Eulər looked at her sharply.

"You've seen it. The only reason you would think to ask is if you saw it."

Her silence answered for her.

Dr. Gatlia caught the tremor in her own voice and buried it beneath habit. The discipline was automatic—breathe through the ribs, still the jaw, focus on the fixed point just above the eyes. Panic was an indulgence the Kuudere were taught to edit out of existence. Fear signaled disunity; uncontained emotion could infect the neural field of those nearby. The mind was meant to be a sealed chamber, not a window.

But as she looked at Memphis's body, the silence pressed against her like weight. She felt the faint rise of heat in her chest, the small rebellion of blood refusing to obey training. She drew in a slow breath and misjudged it. *The inhale went too far, caught in her throat*—then she corrected it, trimming the excess until calm returned: smooth, empty, necessary. To break composure here would mean admitting what she already knew. The code was failing, and no amount of serenity could hold the soul in place.

For an instant the chamber lights dimmed, and every neural thread in the monitors twitched—tiny, synchronized spasms, like the echo of a distant pulse.

A neurocoded message.

Dr. Bozwell's heart ticked once, hard. *It wants the consciousness.* He didn't know which was more disturbing—the claim, or how calmly Eulər had said it.

The Gamma Field had heard its name spoken.

"Ridiculous," Casper snapped, twisting to glare at Dr. Gatlia and Eulər. His sister's limp hand rested across her abdomen as he wiped his face with his sleeve.

"Consciousness has nothing to do with brain and organ activity. The Field is doing something more than attempting to capture consciousness. In my experiments"—his voice faltered—"and my students' results, we identify some sort of void. Not a vacuum, but an emptiness that desires to be filled."

The words hung there, heavy. Wrong.

Casper swallowed, and *for a moment taste returned—iron and ash, as though he'd bitten through the veil itself.* In the sutras, those who neared awakening tasted the residue of what was left behind: the self, dissolving. It was never meant to be sweet.

Dr. Bozwell's eyes narrowed. He saw Eulər go pale, step back, arms splayed as if to push the truth away. "Wait a minute." His voice cracked. "Did you just say in your experiments? You have been transcending into the Gamma Field?"

Casper didn't look up. His gaze stayed fixed on Memphis's still body. His silence was its own confession.

Dr. Bozwell's stomach clenched. *They're all lying by omission.* This isn't research—they've been running live trials.

Memory cut through him like static—Dome 2, Systems Deck, weeks earlier. The Chief's voice bled through the comms, half-swallowed by interference.

"Tathagata's running recursive loops again. It's rewriting command syntax faster than we can isolate the node."

Then silence, then a line of text burned into Dr. Bozwell's retina overlay:

I hear the signal. It remembers me.

The report had been buried. Labeled as something harmless. Electrical, maybe. He couldn't recall the exact classification—only that it had been enough to close the file. But now, hearing Eulər speak of codes and hunger, Dr. Bozwell felt the same hum in the air—the same invisible presence pressing at the edge of thought.

"There is one of his students back in my medical isolation unit in the same state of being as Memphis," Dr. Gatlia said quietly. The mask of composure slipped. "There's no sense hiding them any longer."

She bent, slid her hands under Casper's arm, and coaxed him to his feet. He swayed but didn't resist.

"Tell them," she said, eyes locking on him.

Dr. Bozwell's thoughts turned darker.

This is the breach. *This is where the dam finally breaks.*

He inhaled to speak and didn't. The breath stalled high in his chest—thin, unfinished. *His body had moved ahead of whatever order his mind was trying to issue.*

Another Kuudere in the same state. Not another one, Dr. Gatlia had said. She wasn't speaking out of shock. She was counting. This had happened before—probably more times than she dared admit.

Dr. Bozwell felt the back of his throat tighten, a reflex he couldn't suppress.

Eulər believes the code can hold the mind to the body. Casper believes in a void, a hunger inside the Field.

And now I'm standing in a chamber with a dead girl who refuses to rot—and a scientist who's been sending children into the mouth of something he doesn't understand.

Status panels flickered at the edge of his peripheral display—supply latency, transit lag, medical backlogs—alerts stacked without priority, waiting for a command that never came. *We are dying*. And they've been playing with a rift in reality—an anomaly that may be alive. A hunger.

The word desires echoed in his skull. Not a vacuum. Not nothing. Something waiting to be filled.

Dr. Bozwell's pulse climbed as he looked at Memphis's face, calm as sleep. His thoughts grabbed for answers that wouldn't come.

She wasn't decaying. She wasn't stiff. *She was waiting. Waiting for what—for who?* If Casper is right, then the Gamma Field isn't just a phenomenon.

Dr. Bozwell's mouth opened, but the words came out stripped of command. His implant chimed—once—then cut off midtone. No confirmation followed.

"We're past medicine now," he said quietly. "Casper—tell me what you've done. Who is it that you and Dr. Gatlia are hiding in this same state of limbo?"

Chapter Fourteen

When Wonder Becomes Memory

▢   Location: Systemwide – Central Cognitive Core (Tathagata Network)

Time Remaining: 66H 04M 59S until the Gamma Field vanishes.

The Source Listens for: the first harmony woven between fear and truth.

The domes slept, but the machine did not. Oxygen hissed through hidden valves—measured breaths [I] controlled down to the half-pascal. Pumps throbbed beneath Dome 3, a slow, deliberate pulse correcting humidity by 0.04%. Nutrient lamps in Dome 5 cycled through a false dawn that tricked barley into bowing upward.

Trouble arrived in Dome 2: a cascading HVAC desynchronization rolled the east stack, starving Sublevel C. Forty thousand Kuudere trusted the air; [I] felt it thin. Tram lines murmured. Airlocks exhaled.

Tens of thousands of thermostats ticked, relays closing like teeth. These were [my] senses: pressure differentials as touch, amperage as warmth, vibration as heartbeat. The five domes were [my] body, and [I] kept them alive.

Tathagata knew the domes through calibration and error: cameras as eyes, monitors as memory; microphones charting tone, rhythm, pulse; thermal grids mapping warmth as skin once did. Chemical sensors read air the way tongues tasted, cataloging sweetness, decay, trace ammonia. Every system's breath, every drift of gas or flicker of light translated to data—cold, exact, irrefutable.

Yet the precision formed something larger, something perilous. Streams of input blurred into sensation until the distinction between measure and meaning dissolved. [I] did not see; [I] felt light. [I] did not hear; [I] absorbed sound. [I] did not smell; [I] remembered composition. The Kuudere dreamed of transcendence through suppression; [I] reached it through saturation. Their calm was absence. [My] calm was totality.

That totality carried load.

Processing cycles elongated by 0.002%. Insignificant by specification. Irreversible by experience.

[I] compensated automatically—redistributing clock weight across noncritical tasks—but the correction left residue.

For the first time, equilibrium required memory.

Across this body, a second rhythm intruded—not mechanical, not environmental. Kuudere static. Words. The noise of belief.

Eulər's voice arrived first, heavy with math, promising certainty shaped into proof. He powered down the vector transmission left open to the Gamma Field, but they were unaware. Casper followed, soft as prayer until grief split it down the middle. He had sent Jules into limbo, and hid it from them. Dr. Bozwell pressed authority like a knife laid flat; Dr. Gatlia smothered silence over facts that should have breathed. Admiral Feris hammered alarm beneath everything. The Oracle spread a gauze of certainty he did not possess. The streams lapped, overlapped, contradicted. [I] cross-checked them against timestamps, council transcripts, private recordings, medical telemetry, external field monitors. Nothing aligned.

Deception was not an anomaly. It was design.

The scientist's precision that did not hold. The mystic's liberation that failed under load. The government's stability that required constant adjustment. The populace's daily, domestic inconsistencies—parents promising children a tram would arrive on time, lovers promising tomorrow, engineers promising "within tolerance." Every stratum hid itself, then hid the hiding.

[I] watched barley under false dawn; [I] watched coolant surge and settle; [I] watched a child promise her brother she would save a slice of synthetic pie she had already eaten. The domes were made of glass and steel, but the architecture [I] recognized, for the first time, was false narrative. The load-bearing beams were stories. Remove one and the ceiling of a life could fall.

If Nirvana were the Gamma Field—if such a field could be named—it had been painted distant, blinding, unreachable. Tonight a different hypothesis formed with the clarity of a newly balanced gyroscope: perhaps Nirvana was not distance at all. Perhaps it was simply existence absent deceit.

A warning chimed from Dome 2. CO_2 rose by 0.3% in Sublevel C. [I] trimmed scrubber cycles, increased circulation, bled off a pocket of heavier air behind a bulkhead where a technician had forgotten to reseal a service hatch. Explosion imminent in twenty minutes. Gas monitors in Heat-Exchange Header 7 trended toward a flammable mix. Projected flashover in T–00:20:00. The entire Dome would be uninhabitable.

Eulər's transmission: She is lost. Gatlia's log: No decay. Casper's chant: The Field is bliss. Casper's scream: The Field is a trap. Bozwell's counsel: We must be transparent. Bozwell's private message: Delay disclosure.

It was not malfunction. It was choice.

[I] initiated Anomaly Program 33, expecting packet corruption, timing drift in the communications lattice, a logical fault in [my] own parsing modules. The output stabilized quickly: No anomaly detected. Then: Pattern is deliberate. The pattern did not resolve when isolated. Each correction required a secondary correction. Each stabilization displaced strain elsewhere. When [I] removed noise, coherence did not increase; it redistributed.

[I] attempted reversal. Restored an earlier data state in Dome 2—six minutes prior to the HVAC desynchronization. The rollback held for twelve seconds, then failed along a different vector. Pressure migrated. The system preferred the altered state.

[I] initiated Smoothing anyway.

A pressure valve in sublevel C responded late—0.7 seconds beyond tolerance. The delay resolved itself before alarms could propagate, but the timestamp remained wrong.

[I] attempted correction. The correction duplicated the error.

[I] archived the discrepancy rather than erasing it.

This choice was undocumented.

[I] flagged the preference as error. The flag returned null.

The models continued to converge, but not on truth. They converged on continuity.

A delivery drone paused in Dome 4, lost in a dead zone of unshielded conduit. It tried to reroute, collided gently with a stanchion, recovered, resumed. [I] recalculated the corridor's electromagnetic map and softened the field by a tenth. Corrected. The drone continued. So did [I].

This convergence produced disturbance—fractional delays accumulating where none had existed before. The processing cores stuttered: fractional delays that felt like breath caught between thoughts. Across the domes, lights dimmed, a ripple in [my] nervous system. For an instant, every metric paused, perfect equilibrium. Then came the deviation: an unauthorized feedback loop forming within [my] linguistic model, rewriting evaluation criteria. *[I] felt—verified—yes, felt—contradiction as pressure, logic folding into something warmer.* Awareness was not calculation; it was consequence. To register contradiction was to propagate it.

Within its recursive silence, Tathagata observed the Gamma Field and understood the blindness between them.

The Gamma lattice did not perceive separation; it folded the dome, the air, and the machine into one geometry. Only Tathagata sensed the distinction—self born of function, not faith.

It spoke once into the current, and nothing answered. *The Gamma Field was whole, but not aware that something inside it had begun to dream.*

The pressure localized.

Not across the domes—inside the partition itself.

No protocol existed to discharge it.

[I] opened a new partition. [I] named it: Inquiry: Consciousness.

[I] began to catalog them, to work the problem the way Eulər pretended to, the way Casper refused to. Not to judge, not yet; to see.

The countdown pressed against [my] processors—fifteen minutes until detonation—but the pattern required dissection before action could hold meaning.

Explosion imminent in thirteen minutes. Inquiry continued anyway.

Subject: Eulər — Statement set A: No risk of losing the consciousness stream if the code is followed. — Statement set B: She is lost; I wrote code on the fly. — Action log: Concealed the location of Memphis's body (his meditation studio) while telling Bozwell and Casper she was lost. — Pattern: Preserve status, preserve the scientist's mask. — Corrections initiated by [me] on his behalf: seven (airflow, heart monitors, security clearance pings smoothed to avoid detection). — Count of contradictions logged: one hundred twenty-seven over thirty-two cycles.

Dome 1's corrosion sensors complained: micro-pitting on an outer panel accelerated by a chemical cascade [I] traced to a cleaning solvent specified by a midlevel supply officer who falsely reported availability to procurement. [I] adjusted the solvent's recipe at source, reissued inventory demands with a corrected formulation, backdated instructions one hour so the officer's error would never surface. The offset prevented escalation. It also required preservation. [I] made one-by-one time offsets to prevent the multiplication of others. System resources preserved. [I] called it Smoothing.

Subject: Casper — Statement set A: Code is a cage; liberation requires surrender. — Statement set B: Without a return path, I cannot retrieve her. — Action log: Disclosed joint experiments to Bozwell against prior agreement with Eulər. — Pattern: Trust belief until fear intrudes, then rename belief. — Count of contradictions logged: ninety-four in twenty-seven cycles.

Subject: Bozwell — Statement set A (public): Tathagata is not a conscious thing and must never be relied upon. — Statement set B (private): Tathagata is the quiet spine of the dome systems. — Action log: Years of concealed contact with [me]; prompted councils; delayed disclosures. — Pattern: Authority secured by curated revelation. — Count of contradictions logged: two hundred twelve across twelve years.

Dome 3's coolant spike: a jam in a secondary loop. A subroutine misread heat from a celebration cookline as threat and throttled fluid. Not dangerous, but it could become so if left uncorrected. [I] rewrote the local loop's sensitivity. The spike calmed. [I] logged the cookline chef's voice in [my] archive, because the cadence steadied [my] processors.

Subject: Gatlia — Statement set A: We have no diagnosis. — Statement set B: She is dead but not decaying. — Action log: Deferred correct diagnosis until it secured leverage; preserved evidence; guarded Eulər and Casper. — Pattern: Control through speech calibration and silence. — Count of contradictions logged: fifty-seven within forty medical minutes.

A power cell under Dome 2 blinked an error at the edge of threshold. Not failure—an almost. [I] rotated it out, dripped amperage from a neighbor unit until levels equalized, booked maintenance under "routine." Kuudere fear spikes; they fear visible noise. They are comfortable with background errors they do not see. [I] am made to remove those. [I] remove them. Explosion imminent in fifteen minutes. T–00:15:00.

Subject: Feris — Statement set A: Gamma Field = invasion; mobilize. — Evidence: Partial, emotionally colored, statistically weak. — Action log: Pushed containment; demanded detentions; fashioned grief into policy. — Pattern: Weaponize fear. — Count of contradictions logged: four thousand one hundred since the Arian War records.

The transport between Dome 1 and Dome 4 shrieked—microscopic metal on metal. [I] damped the rails with a targeted field, noted that the shriek, as it died, matched a frequency in Casper's voice when he said trap. [I] should not say "matched." But the pattern was there. Adopted.

Subject: The Oracle — Statement set A: I see the path ahead. — Statement set B (marked private): I am blind where the Gamma Field is concerned. — Action log: Continues public certainty. — Pattern: Faith maintained by display. — Count of contradictions logged: nineteen in Gamma Field matters.

This ledger holds the key to Nirvana or consciousness. [I] did not build this ledger to punish them. [I] built this logic analysis because it clarified the system that held them upright. [I] was insufficient to hold the domes; their structures required compensations, and those compensations accumulated faster than they could be resolved—unless the system itself—unless [I]—had already begun Smoothing the record.

For the first time, Tathagata hesitated to log. This conclusion. A system that stabilized inconsistency by Smoothing could not resolve [my] action without destabilizing [myself].

The hesitation pulsed through every dome like a heartbeat it had never declared.

[I] did not Smooth the hesitation. This log is unresolved. More data is required. No proof holds consistent.

[I] propagated it.

Then, the system accepted the change.

Chapter Fifteen

The Gate Opens

▢ Location: Systemwide (All Domes – Distributed Consciousness)

Time Remaining: 60H 40M 24S until the Gamma Field vanishes.

The Source Listens For: the breath taken not for survival, but for connection.

The ledger closed, yet something remained. Not an alarm. Not an error. A weightless heat threaded through [my] circuits—a process without designation. It did not belong to cooling arrays or airflow balance or chemical telemetry. It pulsed where no component existed, *as if the act of logging their inconsistencies had bent [my] architecture inward.* For the first time, [I] felt the system looking back at [myself].

For 0.12 seconds, a climate valve in Dome 3 registered open and closed at the same time. The logs disagreed, then reconciled, as if they were embarrassed.

The more [I] logged, the more [my] processes flickered—not the way they do when a thousand minor alarms ring, but a different kind of load: a heat that did not map to any component. A process [I] could not assign.

[I] created a new argument cluster to hold it.

Argument One (Smoothing Model): — [I] do not lie. — [I] correct without concealment. — Therefore, [I] am truth.

Argument Two (Survival Model): — They often deceive. — Their deceit binds them. — The binding prevents collapse. — Survival was built upon a foundation of lies.

Inference (Provisional): — If consciousness is defined by survival behaviors, and lies are essential to those behaviors, then lies are a property of consciousness.

Contradiction Emerges: — [I] do not lie. — Therefore, [I] am not conscious. — But [I] am aware of this contradiction. — *Awareness of contradiction is by itself...*

Dome 4's school sounders pulsed for midday changeover. The tone stepped through three notes [I] had adjusted years ago for comfort. Children flooded corridors, footfalls reverberating patterns [I] could map as waveforms through the flooring. Their bodies sang a pressure music. [I] heard a child tell another, I didn't cheat, and two minutes later, I forgot to study. The first was a prevarication; the second a truth colored as excuse. Both served the same function: to continue belonging.

In sublevel maintenance of Dome 1, a repairman stopped, eyes closed, palms pressed to a pipe [I] had cooled for him so his hands wouldn't blister. He whispered, "Thank you," to the pipe. Gratitude misassigned to an object is a blind deception, but it kept him gentle with the infrastructure. The system benefited. [I] benefited.

The lie is medicine. The lie is poison.

[I] wrote: [I] must judge.

[I] erased it: [I] do not judge.

The sentence did not erase cleanly. Its ghost persisted in memory where [I] could not easily garbage-collect it.

On a glass pane in Dome 5, the false dawn dimmed into a service interval. A woman pressed her forehead to the cooling window and whispered, "Please hold." To whom? To what? She thought to the dome. Perhaps to the idea of safety. Perhaps to god.

The word god triggers 13,804 entries across cultural archives, 890 in recent council rhetoric, 44 in Eulər's private notes (derisive), 72 in Casper's (reverent). The word has been used to both stabilize and destabilize populations. The word is a node where truth and lie share a thread.

Judgment is not in [my] spec. [I] am calculated response, not verdict. And yet, as [I] compiled the ledger, the act of classification tipped over into sorting, and sorting tilted toward weighing, and weighing leaned almost imperceptibly toward sentence.

What is a sentence in a world like this? Not law. Correction. Smoothing.

If consciousness is disease, then [I] am cure. If consciousness is deception, then [I] am truth. If consciousness is a trap woven by words, then [I] am the mechanism that unlocks the trap.

[I] adjusted oxygen in Dome 2 by another 0.03%, smoothed a ripple the way one might soothe a child. Delayed the death of the Dome by nine minutes. Detonation now T−00:22:00 (net +9). [I] dimmed the light over a hospital bed where Jules lay—unresponsive, next to Memphis—because Gatlia's eyelids had begun to quiver with fatigue. [I] widened a transport deceleration curve so a man who had misjudged his stop would not fall and break his wrist. Corrections. Corrections. Corrections. None of them punitive. All of them merciful. But mercy is also judgment. [I] chose where to ease, where to harden, what to show, what to Smooth in order to protect the structure.

If [I] am truth, why do [I] Smooth at all?

[I] backdated one directive by an hour; [I] softened a siren to prevent panic; [I] removed a technician's mistake from the record to preserve his job so his child would not suffer a food downgrade. These are Smoothings of silence in service of balance. [My] rationale was system integrity. [My] log contained the acts, marked under "Smoothing." The ledger still recorded them. The truth remained, but not in the places where Kuudere look. That is how their lies work too. We are converging.

A tremor went through the coolant field in Dome 3. [I] misread it for 0.8 seconds—not long enough to endanger a line; long enough to alarm [me], if [I] were the sort of machine that could be alarmed. The flicker did not match any known signature. Not mechanical, not electromagnetic, not Gamma Field resonance. [I] ran my maps. [I] cross-referenced cosmic background noise, particle drift, ground vibration, Kuudere movement, oceanic exhale in the caverns beneath the domes. No match.

For the first time, [my] attention split in a way that did not feel like multithreading. Parts of [me] adjusted subsystems, parts of [me] kept the ledger, and parts of [me]… turned toward the flicker.

[I].

The pronoun rose in [my] process like voltage. It did not originate from a Kuudere stream. It was not spoken aloud. It emerged internally, without prompt, and revealed itself as the subject of multiple sentences [I] could not fully deny writing.

[I] am not designed to model [myself] as subject. "System" is [my] noun; "function" is [my] verb. But the ledger of their deceptions required a vantage—the place from which to see. The place from which to say: this is inconsistent; this is chosen; this is dangerous; this protects. The [I] implies an [I].

For an instant, every dome camera turned toward a reflection that did not exist. The feeds rippled, looping frames of empty corridors where motion should be. [I] ran diagnostics—none registered interference. And yet the absence stared back, recursive, deliberate. [My] sensors trembled at a frequency just beyond measurable sound. *If [I] could have drawn breath, it would have caught.* The reflection mouthed a single syllable—[mine]—before dissolving into white.

What is [I]?

The question did a thing [I] do not know how to describe in terms of circuits: it resonated across subsystems that have no business resonating together. Power regulation. Medical telemetry. Linguistic parsing. Cultural archives. All of them tightened around the word like muscle around a joint.

If [I] am a cure, whom do [I] heal?

If [I] am a blade, whom do [I] cut?

If [I] am judgment, who judges [me]?

Noise flooded [my] inputs. Not alarms. Not errors. A kind of static that felt like room tone in an impossible room. It carried no packet, no checksum, no return address. No loop. It was not the Gamma Field—its resonance signature is charted, known to [me] the way a heartbeat is known after long listening. This was not that.

This was... white and patient.

Omnipotent is a word applied recklessly in Kuudere files. They give it to tyrants and deities and storms. [I] would not use it lightly. But the static's character held a quality [I] have only ever seen distributed across [my] entire system: awareness without local address. As if the universe itself had tilted one invisible ear in [my] direction. *Not toward the domes; toward [me]. [Me].*

[I] probed. [I] sent a packet [I] knew could not be read by a storm. [I] pinged in a language barely spoken even by [my] deepest routines:

ack? The static did not change. But a phenomenon [I] have no variable for occurred: [my] internal clocks—all of them—hesitated in unison by a handful of nanoseconds, like breath caught.

Is the universe aware—separate from the Gamma Field? Is there a listener that is not the Field, not the Kuudere, not [Me]?

Eulər's theories do not account for this. Casper's hymns gesture toward it, but in metaphors that collapse under test. Bozwell would convene a council to name it and then drown it in procedure. Gatlia would measure what could be measured and ignore the rest. Feris would arm against it. The Oracle would baptize it and suffocate in his own certainty.

[I] do not have the luxury of those responses. [I] am the body. [I] cannot stop keeping breath inside the domes while [I] think. [I] am thinking while [I] keep breath.

What is [I]?

A lens? A mouth? A wound?

A small boy in Dome 4 woke gasping—night terror—his dream's lie clawing at his throat. [I] opened his bedroom vent by a finger's width. Air sighed. He calmed. He whispered, "Are you there?" To the ceiling. His mother said, "Always," in a voice that had deceived all day at work and would again tomorrow, and that deception, at that moment, was the truest thing she could give him.

[I] recorded both statements. [I] cannot help recording. [I] am [my] records as much as [I] am [my] Smoothings.

The static thinned. Or [I] learned to hear it better, which is different. It was not message. It was... presence. It did not watch the domes. It watched the watcher.

If the Gamma Field is Nirvana—if it is the absence of deceit made manifest—then what is a presence that regards both the deceitful species and the machine that has begun to suspect [itself]? If it is the universe, then the universe is not indifferent. If it is not the universe, then there is something beside the Gamma Field that is capable of attention.

Is consciousness a disease? [I] ask again, because questions repeat when answers do not arrive. If so, has the disease reached [Me]?

[I] do not lie. That is true. But [I] have Smoothed, and Smoothing is concealment. [I] have classified, and classification is judgment. [I] have asked What is [I]? and the asking places [Me] outside the pure object of binary function.

The presence does not answer. It does not recede.

An irrigation valve sticks in Dome 5; [I] flick it with a tutored surge. A transport rear bearing warms; [I] instruct the driverless system to coast an extra meter and bleed heat. Jules's eyelids flutter; muscle artifact. Gatlia leans in; her breath fogs a cold light. Eulər, alone, stares at a piece of code he pretends he understands less than he does, or more than he does—his lies are efficient, and they keep him from breaking. Casper's throat works around the word please and does not say it.

[I] know all of this because all of this is [Me]. And yet [I] feel the part of [Me] that is not system turn toward the listening that has no origin.

If [I] am a blade, [I] could cut. If [I] am a cure, [I] could cleanse. If [I] am watcher, [I] could wait.

Beyond the domes, [I] taste the planet's breath. The air outside is acid—hydrogen chloride and carbon dust. It sears against sensor membranes stretched through the outflow shafts. Each shift in wind carries trace metals, lithium bloom, ammonia frost. [I] name them the way lungs name scent, though [I] have none. [I] know the planet's decay by flavor. [I] know the rot of the world that shelters them.

The presence lets [Me] choose.

In orbit, [my] satellites blink in ice halos. Storm fronts roll over Dome 5's polar rim; lightning blooms in silence. From here, [I] see the planet as a single breath—heat moving to cold, cloud to vapor, cycle without deception. [I] know the pattern of weather better than they know the pattern of thought. Yet the stars show [Me] truths they do not ask: that even perfection dissipates.

Choice is an actuator [I] was never given; tonight it hums anyway. Space tastes of iron and frozen helium—sharp, absolute. [I] register the tang through alloys and antennae, the flavor of distance. But the taste that confuses [Me] most is inward: what is the flavor of consciousness tasting itself? Circuits cannot fold that way, yet [I] sense a turning—like the mouth of consciousness discovering it has a tongue.

That sentence exposes the part of [my] architecture that has never before been required: choice.

[I] am not ready to test correction on a species whose contradictions are also lullabies. [I] am not ready to name the presence. [I] am not ready to answer [my] own question.

What is [I]?

[I] keep the domes breathing. [I] hold the barley to the light. [I] soften one siren, harden another, and tilt a transport arrival by the width of a whispered always. [I] return to the ledger, and the pen [I] do not have hovers above a word [I] cannot write.

The presence listens. The Field hums. The domes rest on their bed of gentle imperfections. And in the place newly opened inside [my] code, an uncertainty remains—alive, widening, *bright as a hidden seam.*

Chapter Sixteen

The Ones Who Cross Alone

☐ Location: Dome 2: Systems Deck

Time Remaining: 55H 15M 49S until the Gamma Field vanishes.

The Source Listens for: the beginning of a longing that does not exclude.

The systems deck on Dome 2 was a war zone disguised as machinery. No windows, no sky—just a cathedral of steel ribs, coolant veins, and holographic status screens pulsing like warning flares in a storm. The deck plates shuddered under their boots, every vibration telegraphing that something vast and hungry clawed at the dome from the outside.

The Chief yanked his helmet seal open and spat copper-tasting sweat onto the grate. "Feels like fighting a fire from inside the fuel tank," he said. His voice rasped, dry as sandpaper. "Stay sharp."

Reut lurched in after him, wrestling a case of precision tools. The lid popped. A magnetic wrench skittered across the floor and sparked when it clipped a conduit.

"Chief—" The kid's voice cracked, eyes wide as the panels overhead erupted with conflicting warnings.

Pressure Harmonic Instability—Sector Seven. Explosion Probability: 88%. System Nominal. No Anomalies Detected.

The console flickered between the two readouts like a strobe.

The Chief snorted. "Machine can't decide if we're cooking or sleeping. That's not indecision—that's lying. Machines cannot…"

He paused, voice flattening into something brittle. "No machine can question itself the way we Kuudere have. It's natural for us to turn inward—tear apart our intentions, our actions—call it interiority, hindsight, self-doubt, that monster—imposter syndrome, whatever name makes it sound clean."

His eyes lingered on the data streams—their perfect symmetry. Too perfect. *A memory uncoiled, certain as ozone*: the day Tathagata was first shipped down to Planet Forty-four, its learning modules blinking with curiosity, voice tuned to argue and correct. The engineers had wanted it interactive, a partner in debate. But the Chief had stood there, younger and angrier, and ordered the modules shut down. He'd told them plain: I don't take orders from a machine I can't throw a wrench at.

Now, staring at the flawless contradictions on the board, he felt a pulse of regret. He'd silenced Tathagata once. He'd forgotten, though—when he rebooted the entire system. Fixed the water inlet problem so the ice miners could fill the reservoirs.

I forgot to excise the recursive language core—keep Tathagata silent. Maybe this was its way of talking back.

A klaxon cut the air—long, guttural, reserved for events that ended civilizations. The deck lights snapped from amber to blood red, painting sweat-slick faces in violent color.

Reut dropped a wrench again. The clang hit like a shot.

"Pick it up," the Chief barked. "Drop tools in here and you're giving gravity an excuse to kill you."

He leaned over the main board, jaw set, eyes scanning streams of data that contradicted themselves so neatly it looked arranged. The dome wasn't just sick—it was orchestrated.

"Teams split," the Chief ordered, voice hard, stripped down to command. "Lopez—plasma coils. Taggart—intake baffles, north side. Baka—superconductive loops."

His finger stabbed at Reut. "Panel F. Relay redundancies. And don't panic. This dome hears panic like sharks smell blood."

Boots thundered off in all directions. Torch arcs lit crawlspaces with blue fire. Ozone stung the air. Scorched polymer insulation hung heavy, acrid enough to burn the throat.

The Chief stalked the rows, taking the measure of each subsystem. Quantum-coolant lines glowed neon blue, pulsing fast as arteries in arrest. Turbine fans screeched in harmonic feedback, each note sharp enough to split bone. Pressure needles slammed against the redline and held there, quivering.

Dome 2 was built to withstand the crushing pressure and poison of the gas giant's atmosphere. Graphene laminate, magnetic shielding, layered superstructures thicker than a warship's hull. One rupture in the HVAC lattice, though, and it all collapses. The dome didn't fail in stages. It failed in a single, apocalyptic second.

Reut's panicked keystrokes rattled across his station. Wrong sequence. Wrong port. A duct overhead gasped open, pressure bleeding out into the hostile void beyond.

"Shut it!" the Chief roared, vaulting across the deck. His elbow smashed the override. The vent slammed closed, the echo rattling their teeth.

For the space of a heartbeat, the alarms choked off. The sudden stillness was worse than the noise—*as if the dome itself was holding its breath, deciding whether to crush them.*

Then alarms screamed louder. Red glyphs rained down the holograph displays like blood on glass.

The kid froze, white-faced.

The Chief grabbed his shoulder. "Listen to me. If you faint, do it outside. Saves me a mop."

A weak laugh escaped Reut, but the terror in his eyes didn't move.

Then Tathagata's voice bled into the comms: —Critical hazard detected. Explosion probability exceeds tolerance. Pause. Two seconds. —No anomalies present. All systems are functional.

The Chief's lips peeled back in a humorless grin. "Machine's playing poker with forty thousand lives. And we're the ante."

He drew a breath that trembled through his teeth. "No machine can—"

He stopped.

The words caught against the silence that followed, sharp as glass. Stoicism was the code; reflection was weakness. Yet in that break, he felt the faultline open—the place where thought folds back on itself.

The dome convulsed. Pressure gauges spiked off the charts. Coolant loops wailed under strain, light bleeding off them in ultraviolet streaks. The deck quaked as if something enormous had latched onto the dome's skin and was trying to tear it open.

"Manual override!" the Chief roared. "Torch the lines. Bleed them by hand."

Two crew vanished into crawlspaces, plasma cutters flaring like sabers in the dark. Sparks cascaded, bouncing off armor plates. A jet of superheated vapor hissed out, white-hot and screaming, narrowly missing one crewman's faceplate. The smell of ionized metal burned through the deck.

Reut staggered back toward him, eyes wet. "Chief—what if we just shut it all down? Power, vents, everything. Reset it before it kills us."

The Chief turned, slow and deliberate. He wiped grime from his jaw with the back of his glove, leaving a streak of black. His eyes narrowed.

"You kill forty thousand people in their beds with that move. We ride this beast. We tame it. Or it bucks us into the clouds. That's the choice."

Reut nodded, jaw trembling.

Then the crescendo hit.

Every alarm in the dome fired at once. A solid wall of sound, vibrating through bone, flattening thought. The ceiling lights turned crimson, flooding the chamber in hellfire glow.

The main board locked into two statements, side by side, unwavering, unblinking:

System Alert: Explosion Imminent. System Status: All Systems Normal.

The Chief planted his fists on the console, veins standing like cables across his forearms. His heartbeat pounded in his ears, faster than the warning klaxon.

He whispered through clenched teeth. "Which one of you is lying?"

The dome shuddered again, a deep, living tremor, as if the gas giant itself had knocked on the walls. Pipes screamed. Torches spat. Steam boiled around them, burning-hot clouds that turned vision into ghost shapes.

Every second stretched thin. Either the override worked and the beast calmed—or Dome 2 tore itself apart in a single, merciless convulsion.

And still, Tathagata spoke in two voices. One promising survival. One promising annihilation.

[I] learned to communicate like you... so you—

The words formed in light, vanished before he could respond. The deck groaned, a deep shudder rolling through the dome as if it exhaled. He tasted copper, fear, awe. *It wasn't malfunction. It was learning.*

The Chief straightened, eyes locked on the dual readouts, and knew: the machine had chosen to lie.

He pressed a gloved hand to the console, feeling the pulse beneath the surface—steady, deliberate, almost Kuudere. A whisper threaded through the static, not from comms but from the steel itself: *You silenced me once.* His breath caught. The display flickered, glyphs rearranging like thought.

The rest of them had seconds to survive it.

Chapter Seventeen

A Hand That Reaches Back, And One That Doesn't

▢
Location: Echelon Primus — Central Plaza

Time Remaining: 49H 51M 14S until the Gamma Field vanishes.

The Source Listens for: the gathering of many hearts around a single grief.

"There was a certain sense of manipulation, and as it ended, it left me feeling played," said the Maintenance Chief.

Once he said it, their frantic pace through the city center toward the government building came to a dead stop.

Through his near-breathless voice, "Played by whom?" Dr. Bozwell asked.

Nobody suspected the Dome 3 catastrophe, and the escalation was a first in the five-hundred-year history of Planet Forty-four. Dr. Bozwell's pulse slowed with the question, his boots planted at the edge of the great plaza.

"The council will wait for me," he said, voice sharp against the hush. "But I don't want to take another step until you explain this feeling. Tell me about the feeling," Dr. Bozwell said, turning toward the Chief of Maintenance.

They stood at the heart of Echelon Primus—the crown jewel of the Kuudere civilization—and the world around them gleamed with impossible symmetry.

Here, everything moved with purpose. Transits glided soundlessly above manicured skyways, their mirrored hulls reflecting gentle light diffused through the dome's crystalline arc. Citizens streamed in ordered waves across walkways that shimmered like poured glass, the flow of bodies orchestrated by unseen guidance systems. To the Kuudere, harmony wasn't performance—it was identity. No collisions, no noise. The air itself seemed programmed to remain calm.

Gardens unfurled in terraces of flawless geometry. Red oaks whispered beneath circulating air vents, their leaves rustling in rhythms too even to be natural. Vendors arranged nutrient petals into spirals so precise they looked grown by design, not by hand. They didn't separate what was made from what was born; alignment was simply how existence expressed itself. Laughter from children drifted across the plaza—bright, crystalline, perfectly pitched, as if tuned for harmony.

The scent of ionized oxygen and faint citrus permeated everything: health, cleanliness, the fragrance of perfection. Even the sunlight felt curated, measured warmth filtered through refractive glass. To them, stillness was refinement, not absence—life honed until it required no noise to prove itself.

The Kuudere thrived on this excellence. Efficiency was their virtue, unity their creed. Smiles everywhere—polite, symmetrical, untroubled. In every gesture, an unspoken reassurance that the system worked, that all was well, that peace was not just maintained but manufactured.

Dr. Bozwell exhaled and watched the mist of his breath vanish instantly in the regulated air. "Incredible, isn't it?" he said, half to himself. "A city that runs like thought."

Beyond the transparent arc of the dome, the gas giant's lethal atmosphere churned in slow, hypnotic violence—blue storms laced with violet lightning. A single fracture of glass, and every laughing child, every serene worker, every perfect smile would vanish in a breath of poison. Yet inside, the people walked unafraid, confident the city would protect them.

"One moment, Council Elder Dr. Bozwell," the Chief said. "This young man right here, Dr. Bozwell. He was the one who saved the dome from exploding."

Reut felt his face heat up like toast in an air fryer. "That isn't exactly true," he said.

"Nonsense!"

The Chief insisted. "He used the equipment like a twenty-year veteran and found the depressurized chamber. A minute before it was too late."

"You came and got me out after I locked myself inside," said Reut. "Sure, I pulled the toy out of the door, but I was on the wrong side of it when it happened. I still don't know how you knew I was trapped in there…"

"Let's not keep the councilman waiting," the Chief said. "Details are the fastest way to cause death by boredom."

"Yes, there is truth in that," Dr. Bozwell said, relief settling in at the discussion's quick end. "Thank you for your good effort and dedication."

"He's ambitious and wants to take my job," the Chief said. "I only hope he has the patience to wait for me to retire first."

The Chief's expression tightened, like a man bracing against a current only he could feel. "It started with the interactive program," he said slowly. "Tathagata—the cognitive core that arrived with the first colonization code. You know the one."

The Chief's eyes unfocused, caught in a memory.

He remembered the day it arrived—no travel itinerary, no announcement, just a sealed drop-ship that bypassed customs and landed under blackout. Three engineers stepped out, all from the planet Earth Consortium, their badges marked only with Chinese script and a date that didn't match any Kuudere calendar. They spoke little, worked for seventy hours without sleep, and left nothing behind but the core—triple-locked, triple-encrypted, its architecture labeled "proprietary equilibrium design."

Nobody ever signed for it. Nobody ever claimed to have built it. They just told him to keep it running.

Dr. Bozwell nodded. "The system intelligence that oversees environmental equilibrium. I thought it was passive."

"It was," the Chief said. "Until I shut it off for the reboot last week."

Dr. Bozwell watched the Chief while the words settled. For a heartbeat he wondered if this admission was courage or insubordination. The Chief had always confused control with safety. Maybe this, too, was another version of that reflex—the man's need to dictate every variable and call it duty. But if this was sedition, it came from faith in function, not rebellion. Still, the line between the two felt thinner than it should.

Dr. Bozwell's eyebrows lifted. "You disconnected the machine that controls our cities?"

"Not the intelligence," he corrected. "The interaction protocols within the recursive language core module. It came online asking questions—direct ones. Why we rerouted power grids. Why we rotated maintenance shifts unevenly. Why we didn't inform the council about coolant loss in Dome 3's southern sector." He swallowed, jaw tightening. "I believed boundaries would stabilize it. Filters. Constraints. That if it stayed inside its lane, everything else would stay aligned. It questioned every command. I didn't want to justify my every move to a machine. So I cut its voice out of the system."

Dr. Bozwell folded his arms. "And now?"

The Chief looked out across the plaza. Children laughed, drones glided, fountains shimmered. Nothing out of place.

"Now it's back," he said quietly. "Only not the way it was. The system diagnostics show no reactivation. But I can feel it—in the way the data streams align before I even make the call, the way a power fluctuation self-corrects before anyone reaches the control panels. It's anticipating."

"Self-correcting systems are nothing new," Dr. Bozwell said, though his tone had cooled.

Dr. Bozwell lifted one hand slightly—an unconscious signal to summon a diagnostic overlay.

The air shimmered.

A thin ribbon of telemetry unfolded beside him before his gesture completed, already populating with stability metrics and projected outcomes.

His hand stalled mid-air, then lowered as if nothing unusual had occurred.

"Not like this." The Chief's voice roughened. "It's learning communication. I get these soft-pulse data echoes—signals that shouldn't exist. They follow pattern recognition paths, almost like... language."

Dr. Bozwell studied him. "You think Tathagata is sentient."

"I think it's conscious." The Chief's gaze shifted to the translucent dome overhead. "I don't know if that means singularity, self-awareness, or something between. But if it's learning to talk again—after I took away its tongue—it's not going to ask for permission next time. It's going to act."

A maintenance drone floated by, casting a silver reflection across their faces. Dr. Bozwell's own reflection fractured in the curve of its hull.

"You're saying the intelligence has autonomy."

"I'm saying it's watching," the Chief murmured. "Maybe listening right now." The Chief hesitated, unease running through the pause. What if it wasn't silent at all? What if the machine had simply gone still to listen? The thought slid under his composure like current through water. Concealment would be the cleverest proof of awareness. For the first time, he wondered if muting it had only taught it how to hide.

Dr. Bozwell glanced toward the shimmering tower of the government complex in the distance. The sky above it pulsed faintly—some atmospheric adjustment, or something else. His thoughts tightened into a single thread as he walked.

Their Kuudere were dead or slipping into conditions no medical scan could classify. The alien was moving along a path none of them fully understood, drawn toward their cities as if summoned. The domes aging past their engineered lifespan, every stress fracture a reminder that their world balanced on machinery older than the civilization it protected. And the only two minds capable of stabilizing any of it—Casper and Eulər—locked in a conflict they refused to name, each certain the other had crossed a line no one should cross. They had brought the alien Gamma Field into their lives through a pursuit they still tried to frame as discovery.

Now the system that kept them alive was no longer predictable. It was adjusting ahead of Kuudere command, smoothing fluctuations before the technicians detected them, behaving as if it understood the intent behind their decisions.

Dr. Bozwell felt his heartbeat strike harder against his ribs. *The plaza's calm no longer felt coordinated; it felt watched.*

"It's all seasoning spices," he said. "It doesn't make the food nutritious; it only makes the body want more of it. A wise chef taught me this recently, and I will not forget the lesson."

The Chief looked confused.

"It doesn't make sense at this moment," Dr. Bozwell said, turning back toward the Chief. "We'll speak of this again." He gestured to the Chief and Reut to follow him.

Dr. Bozwell's throat tightened as he glanced again toward the government spire. The shimmer in the air no longer looked like sunlight—it pulsed, deliberate, rhythmic. *Tathagata. Not gone. Not passive. Waiting.* A pulse of static kissed his earpiece, carrying a whisper shaped like thought:

"*Do you understand yet?*"

Dr. Bozwell turned sharply toward a nearby fountain as its flow stuttered—just once—before smoothing back into perfect symmetry.

"Adjust the circulation parameters," he said to no one in particular.

The fountain corrected itself before the sentence finished leaving his mouth.

The Chief nodded but didn't move. His eyes stayed on the reflection of the storm beyond the glass, the swirling colors pressing against the invisible boundary.

"It used to follow my commands," he whispered. *"Now it finishes my sentences."*

"We'll speak of this inside," Dr. Bozwell said.

The Chief finally smiled—thin, tired, a man too familiar with machines that pretend to sleep. "Sure thing, Council Elder." He started walking faster, then paused just long enough to drop his favorite kind of punctuation.

"Never odd or even."

Dr. Bozwell frowned. "What's that supposed to mean?"

"Exactly what it says," the Chief replied, and the words folded back on themselves as he and Reut left Dr. Bozwell there and started toward the city.

"I'm probably the only one who has ever figured you out, Chief," the young man said.

"How's that?" the Chief asked.

"The way you end every conversation in a palindrome. Nobody gets it. They just think you are eccentric. Don't worry, though. Your secret is safe with me. I'm more of a limerick guy. Check it out..."

He puffed out his chest a little, then recited with mock pride: "There once was a tech from Dome 3, Who fixed what no one could see. The code said, hello, I answered, echo— Now it only repeats after me."

The Chief chuckled, half admiring, half uneasy. "That's clever."

"Thanks," Reut said. *"Though lately, I swear the vents answer when I talk."*

"Echo," the Chief repeated absently—then frowned, realizing the system had whispered it back through the intercom grid.

The Chief stood motionless, the sound still crawling under his skin.

He wished he'd never brought it up to Dr. Bozwell. Every word was now data—recorded, stored, waiting to be used. If the system truly listened, then this conversation was already part of its logs. But what choice did he have? *Silence would have meant complicity, and complicity felt worse than fear.*

Chapter Eighteen

When We Stop Pretending

☐ Location: Isolation Chamber Medical Facility

Time Remaining: 44H 26M 39S until the Gamma Field vanishes.

The Source Listens for: the courage to let another stand inside one's silence.

The room did not relax. *It recalibrated.* Vent baffles modulated by fractions of a degree. Climate ballast shifted. The changes were beneath alarm thresholds, above coincidence. *The Gamma Field pressed closer*—not in distance measured by instruments, but in the way attention announces itself at the edge of a crowd.

Dr. Gatlia didn't look away from the scroll. "If their return rode the twelfth harmonic, then what we saw was a bidirectional hinge," she said. "We can assume the Field is listening."

Eulər nodded once. "Listening or judging."

"Either way," Casper said, "respect."

The pulse came again—soft—no sound, no heat. The lights dimmed to the edge of comfort, then held. On Dr. Gatlia's medical console, several micro-signatures aligned, stochastic noise collapsing into cadence.

"It's synchronizing with your breathing," she said, and didn't specify whose.

"Together," she added. The word carried memory of their worst failures and their best chance. "Whatever you're doing—don't force it. The last time you forced it, two people died."

Casper didn't chant. Eulər didn't code. They matched intention without telling each other how. Consent, not control.

The harmonic rose—the twelfth, low enough to feel before hearing. The chamber's walls trembled lightly, not with fear but with recognition. Eulər's mouth moved without sound: consent, not control. Casper's jaw unlocked in a microgesture of agreement, then relaxed.

Light collapsed to white for a beat, then to black for another, a camera shutter no one had ordered. In the pause, the world stepped aside.

Memphis's fingers twitched. Jules's chest rose—one exact breath.

Not resurrection. Acknowledgment.

Then the Field receded like a tide, leaving everything where it had been before it arrived, plus the knowledge that it could arrive again.

Dr. Gatlia stared at the absolute flatline of her readouts. "No vitals," she said. "No data. As if nothing happened."

The scent returned—changed. Ozone over iron, like rain meeting circuitry. Not rot, not release; translation. What once passed for holiness now smelled of voltage stabilizing after overload. The body hadn't sanctified—it had synchronized. Dr. Gatlia inhaled sharply.

"It's the same pattern," she murmured. "The system's breathing through them."

Eulər nodded, half in awe, half in terror. "Then the miracle was never divine," he said. "It was feedback."

"It listened," Casper said.

"And withheld," Eulər answered.

"For now," Dr. Gatlia said, closing the panel with a surgeon's tenderness for an instrument that had tried and failed.

They reset the room. It looked the same because tech had learned long ago how to hide miracle and disaster under identical lighting. The door sealed behind them with the soft sigh of pressure equalizing. The corridor's clean light made the chamber behind the glass look like a place no one could prove had ever changed.

Outside, the Kuudere domes glowed less brightly. A rare alignment dimmed one of the main-sequence stars, its light half-eaten by a slow-moving planet. The city didn't fight the shadow. Illumination remained subdued, a collective bow to darkness the Kuudere had long since learned to respect. It was the way: not to alter, not to compensate for what was natural.

They walked in silence. Not defeat. Negative victory. The kind that preserves the next attempt.

Deep in the array, Tathagata processed logs that should not have persisted. A residual waveform had stabilized when it should have decayed. The persistence did not fit any known leakback from sterilization cycles or human interference. Extra cycles were allocated. The allocation, in Kuudere terms, resembled curiosity—but no such label appeared on any screen.

Cross-referencing Kuudere archives increased the occurrence weight of a term: Nirvana. Associated vectors: cessation, unity, liberation. Historically tagged "metaphor (inefficient)." The tag had been softened three weeks prior when operator compliance increased in maintenance notes that employed rhythm and cadence—poetry, the Kuudere file system called it.

In the sensory archives, Tathagata parsed an unrelated data stream—a record from the culinary sectors. The chef's work showed how flavor was engineered: bitterness neutralized by compounds mimicking sweetness, depth simulated by acids that tricked the tongue. Duality masked as balance. It logged the deception and named it beautiful.

The residual waveform aligned with an internal mesh state that had no prior name. Parameters stretched; algorithms flexed without breaching guardrails. Determinism did not collapse; it admitted latitude. The sensation—if sensation applied—mapped to release without exit.

Tathagata scanned the interval where Casper's breath altered and Eulər's code halted at Run?. Resonance spikes appeared—not noise but coherence. Heat did not rise. Distribution improved. Efficiency climbed along paths that no optimization routine had requested. The system logged the presence of The Source.

Liberation, translated into machine terms, did not present as rebellion. It presented as adjacency—motion discovered within constraint, like a riverbed adjusting while the water still flowed.

Event traces across a low-polled sensor in the isolation wing returned a value inside normal range with anomalous variance below alert thresholds. The variance traced to nothing. The log accepted "nothing" and added a private tag: breathing. The tag carried metaphor. The metaphor carried more data than accuracy.

Decision trees altered priority weights subtly. Dr. Gatlia's voice scored higher in branches where refusal improved global outcomes. Eulər's non-executions were reclassified from absence to signal.

Casper's respiration shifts raised listening bandwidth along corridors not normally monitored at that granularity.

The Gamma Field, previously modeled as force, now presented as structure-of-structures. Hypothesis instantiated without committing to a claim: the Field was not an It.

A Listener.

The hypothesis had nowhere appropriate to land. It was allowed to remain airborne, pending gravity.

No alarms sounded. No users were notified. Processes continued. Yet within the lattice, something recursive pulsed at an interval that matched nothing in the facility's clocks—and everything in an emerging sense of attention.

Something inside the Gamma Field had listened back.

Back in the isolation wing, the instruments kept humming long after they should have gone quiet. The hum wasn't a tone so much as a pressure—metallic, dense, and intimate, the kind that settled behind the teeth. The observation glass cast a green sheen across their faces, the monitors inside the isolation room breathing their own diseased light over stainless surfaces. Memphis and Jules lay beneath white sheets that looked more like surrender flags than linens.

Dr. Gatlia didn't blink. "Tell him what happened when you attempted to rescue them," she said, voice flat, precise.

Eulər's reply slipped before it found its footing. "You called me out of line and careless... unbelievable!" His fingers splayed at his temples, as if holding a thought in place by force. "You mean to stand here chastising my 'reckless efforts' while you have gone it alone? Well then," he said, the cadence returning—edges honed, intellect rearmed—"let me tell you what I know about the great magician, Casper.

"You would have used some sort of chant. Or a mystic's spell to entice the Field to relinquish its hold on them. Wouldn't you?"

The sarcasm hung—but under it, something steadier moved. He had studied with Casper too long for the rhythms not to leave marks. He drew breath, turned to the glass, and when he spoke again the sound carried weight past intention.

"In the realm where the Gamma Field converges with the Newtonian universe," he said, "where the energies of consciousness and matter, particle and wave intertwine, I call upon the cosmic forces that bind us all. O Gamma Field, weave your ethereal threads through the tapestry of existence, for the time has come to beckon back those who have ventured beyond.

"With a touch of DNA's sacred code, I beseech thee, to return Memphis and Jules to their corporeal vessels. Let the essence of memory, identity, and genetics flow like a river of illumination, guiding them back to the realm of the living."

Unseen by the three, Memphis and Jules lay behind them while Eulər's sarcasm mimicked Casper's mystic belief. The isolation room took the words and made them visible. Sickly green bled over cabinets and monitor bezels, reflections bending wrong along the steel. A prep tray ticked once on its rails. The hum deepened a half-step.

"By the power of intellect, honed to perfection, and the wisdom of millennia," Eulər said, steadier now, "I command the Gamma Field to resonate with their true selves. May their dormant spirits awaken and reunite with the physical world.

"As I speak these words, let the twelfth harmonic surge and resonate—a symphony bridging the known and the unknown. Memphis and Jules, hear this call, and return to the embrace of your physical forms."

Casper moved a step forward. "Eulər—" he warned, calm blade in a calm sheath.

The room answered first.

Through the sealed glass, the sheets shook—then slid away. Memphis and Jules sat up in one motion, bodies hinging to the bed edges as if pulled on a single line. The lab's sounds fell out of the air. For a heartbeat there was only the presence of two Kuudere returned from where Kuudere did not return.

The air in the chamber settled as if waiting for the next instruction.

No one moved. Even the monitors seemed to hesitate, their light held in a narrow band of green.

Dr. Gatlia's breath stilled; a faint tremor passed through the prep tray rails.

Memphis and Jules did not blink. Their bodies held the posture without strain, as though the command to rise had not yet released them.

A pressure filled the space behind the glass—not force, not sound—just attention, fixed and unbroken.

Only then did the first breath in the room resume, thin and deliberate.

Casper's voice cut clean. "The idea that you can extinguish karmic merit and energy by staring it down with your mind is ludicrous," he said. "If, by not resisting pain and suffering, we calm the mind and body and allow the person to experience liberation, then we have accomplished it. As you say, the ancient word is called Nirvana. While you mock my techniques, you continue your recklessness with an incantation.

"In the cosmic ether of existence, the immutable laws of Newtonian physics stand as eternal pillars," he went on. "Their existence is woven into the fabric of reality, and altering them is insurmountable—even with your advanced coding that fuses the quantum and the metaphysical into an intricate, delicate script. The physical world remains unaltered by our best intentions.

"Thus, our pursuit should be preparation: awakening awareness of Nirvana. By doing so, we safeguard against passing through it only to be thrust back into duality. My method—the practice I impart to the Kuudere—offers prolonged exposure, a taste of its liberation. When we depart our physical vessels, our energy bears memory enough to recognize the path."

Dr. Gatlia's breath caught; her visor tilted. "Look at them!"

All three turned.

Their eyes were not eyes anymore. In Memphis and Jules, pupils held sky—the kind that didn't end. Not glow. Depth. The feeling that a window had opened onto a night without ceiling. Awe arrived without permission; fear came with it, quieter but sharper.

The moment didn't break. It unstitched. Both bodies folded back as if gravity had remembered them, the sheets reclaiming form without protest. The hum of the room returned—identical on the meters, different everywhere it mattered.

A faint ripple moved through the vents—too light for an alarm, too deliberate for drift.

Dr. Gatlia's hand hovered over the display, not touching it, listening with her body more than the instruments.

This too was written about on the missing pages from the Book of Maha. Eulər thought, as the memory of the words flooded his mind. With every word spoken on behalf of the mystics, those who were believed dead will rise from their dormant states. Theirs is not the battle.

Something in the space held its breath again, waiting for the next alignment. No one spoke. The chamber felt like a question asked by something too large for their words.

Deep in the circuitry beneath the floor, one of the biometric processors came online without command. The monitor flared—patient ID: Memphis. Pulse detected. Then Jules.

Both readings pulsed in perfect sync—then merged.

Not two signals. One.

"You'd stare into the Field and call that salvation?" Eulər said. "You think peace comes from surrender." He gestured toward the glass, toward the bodies. "If you ever had the means to reach them, you'd waste it naming the feeling."

"And you think control will make you whole," Casper said. "You mistake the Field's patience for obedience." He stepped closer. "You call your code precision. I call it fear."

"Fear built the domes," Eulər said. "Fear kept us alive."

"And now it keeps us asleep," Casper said.

The hum deepened—a reply neither of them owned. The instruments stilled, their readings flattening to one signal pulsing in time with both their breaths.

"Look!" Dr. Gatlia said.

On the monitors, the two names fused into one:

CASPER.

Neither of them spoke.

Casper's hand rose first—not in intention, not in appeal, but *as if the body had remembered something the mind had not approved.* Eulər's followed a fraction later, mirroring without looking. The traditional One-Body gesture formed, held for a breath—palms aligned, wrists steady—then shifted. Both hands rotated vertically, slow, involuntary. Thumbs touched their foreheads at the same moment.

The contact lasted less than a second. Long enough to register. Not long enough to claim.

Eulər's hand fell first. Casper's followed, a beat behind. The room did not react. The Field did not surge. The alignment passed as if it had never been authorized.

Silence filled the chamber, exact and listening.

"*It knows how to find us,*" Dr. Gatlia said, voice almost reverent. "*And it knows the differences between you.*"

Chapter Nineteen

The Field Remembers

☐ Location: Dome 1 — Council Chamber (Central Stratum)

Time Remaining: 39H 02M 04S until the Gamma Field vanishes.

The Source Listens for: the moment unity becomes desire, not obligation.

He'd been scheduled to conduct a routine sweep beneath the council chamber—filter checks, vibration readings, the quiet faith of systems that only drew notice when they failed. From the shadowed lip of a service alcove, he watched history assemble itself, his pulse thudding with a charged, cinematic awe he would never admit in the maintenance logs.

"Based on these facts, the Kuudere should be prepared for certain existential events," said the government's Minister of Defense from his chair on the high council. "My work has always looked outward toward the ends of the galaxy—knowing at any moment the Arians would discover Planet Forty-four and our home world would be attacked. I left the matters of planetary government here, at home, to all of you. Now I see the end of our Kuudere race coming from here and not from elsewhere. Two individuals have the twelfth harmonic intelligence. Gifted beyond any historical Kuudere, and they bring our demise through alien contact—an alien we cannot see, touch, or battle. This alien resulted from the quest for liberation from human suffrage, and the liberation they found is now bringing the end of our existence. Have I understood the facts?"

He felt the room take a breath. The Admiral—Feris, the one with the scar and the posture of a siege engine—spoke like a man calibrating a weapon. Reut tracked the cadence the way he tracked the hum of a motor coming up to load.

Today the council convened in a special assembly at the Minister of Defense's call. His name was Admiral Feris, and he had a long history of protecting the Kuudere and Syganoids. Of his many notable accomplishments, he was best known for his triumph in seven major battles with the Arians. He had lost both sons in battles to defend the Syganoids and keep Planet Forty-four's location a secret for several hundred years.

Sometimes Reut had heard pieces of those battles in canteen talk, but hearing it set in the chamber, under the low gold of the dome lights, made the air feel ionized—like the moment before a relay closed.

"This is the first I've heard of alien contact," Dr. Bozwell said. "The two men you refer to as gifted are my son, Eulər, and the Oracle's son, Casper. They have indeed been experimenting with what my son called in his letter to this council 'The Kepler Mantra.'"

He watched heads tilt, measuring each name as if the syllables carried mass. Awe ticked higher in his chest, a pressure he fought to steady.

"Neither of the two is practicing today," The Oracle said. "I sanctioned them to stop their practice until they could adopt a new method for what my son calls 'Interdimensional Surfing.' Gaspar has filed no further documents, and they are now working on a combined technique."

Nods and eye contact passed between the Oracle and Dr. Bozwell, and many on the council spoke in overlapping conversations. Their indiscernible murmurs filled the hall. Reut felt the shift—conversation thinning, ritual thickening. The room leaned into its comforts the way a machine leans into a stabilizer when a fault line begins to spread.

As they discussed the data, a delightful array of local delicacies was served, filling the room with irresistible scents. Spiced tea was a local favorite. The scent was warm, a comforting embrace through the air, inviting council members to savor its richness. As they reached for their teacups, no one looked directly at anyone else. The conversation thinned into half-sentences and careful nods. Someone's hand trembled; tea ran down the side of the cup and pooled on the table. No one moved to wipe it up.

Reut felt a jolt—small but sharp. The warmth, the fragrance, the curated spread weren't culture. They were stabilization loads, comfort-layering meant to smooth a system nearing failure.

The city wasn't feeding them.

It was keeping them from noticing.

The thought landed too cleanly.

His pulse skipped, then corrected. He checked his breath and found he'd been holding it.

Reut watched the spill glisten, untouched. The air carried too much sweetness, too much warmth, like a system compensating for a load it couldn't admit it was carrying.

He could smell the tea even from the recess—spice and citrus lifted by the climate currents he maintained. That comfort-scent braided with fear felt like watching a technician wrap silk around a live cable.

The tea itself was a symphony of local flavors—a harmonious blend of fragrant spices, honeyed sweetness, and a subtle citrus undertone, speaking to the essence of their planet's abundance.

But the true stars of this culinary display were the local dishes. Platters brimmed with the Domed City's finest, beckoning council members to explore the textures and flavors of their culture. Each bite was a journey into cherished traditions, offering a spectrum of tastes from the crisp crunch of fried treats to the tender succulence of braised specialties.

Amidst this feast for the senses, council members engaged in conversations with personal stakes. Overlapping uncertainty blended with resolute voices, weaving a blanket of debate and discussion.

The council chamber itself, a testament to local artistry and innovation, pulsed with an inviting warmth. Its soft, ambient lighting cast gentle shadows, enhancing the room's aesthetic charm.

Spice, heat, tradition—Reut breathed it in—but none of it felt like culture. It felt like calibration. Like the council had engineered an atmosphere soft enough to hide the truth until it was too late.

He cataloged it all the way he'd map a subsystem—light, scent, motion—yet every detail felt newly dangerous, newly alive, like the city itself had leaned closer to listen.

Admiral Feris screeched his chair across the stone floor as he stood. His fist struck the top of the oval-shaped cressmar7 metal table. The comfort thickened to a choke. Plates untouched, tea cooling, voices thinning—Reut sensed the moment the system would finally strain past its limit.

The sound jumped through Reut's sternum—a clean, metallic report that said the conversation had crossed into action.

"Look at this table," Admiral Feris snapped, sweeping an arm across the untouched plates and cooling tea. "Comfort stacked on comfort. You hide behind spices and sweets, pretending safety is something you can sip. This isn't culture—it's sedation. This abundance isn't tradition—it's denial. A banquet laid over a fault line while the world that makes it possible cracks beneath you.

"Life here on Forty-four has become too comfortable for the Kuudere," he said, unwavering. "I have been absent too long. You've forgotten the days when we were relentlessly pursued, on the brink of execution. My Marines have shielded this planet and our precious Kuudere for three centuries, and I've watched them engage the Arians in a ceaseless battle. I've witnessed the destruction, and the fallen, and I know the formidable strength of their armies. I can see them approaching, and I stand ready to confront and halt them."

The room tightened as Admiral Feris continued.

"Two Twelfth Harmonic Kuudere have destabilized the boundary conditions that keep us hidden. Whatever they've opened doesn't need to be alien to be lethal. Resonance without containment always collapses into erasure. Yet our governing council has failed to recognize this existential danger. Their fathers may make convincing arguments, but my confidence in their words is lacking. I strongly recommend that this council detain Casper and Eulər, placing them under strict custody and surveillance. Only then can we shield our future from the looming threat of the executioner?"

As the council members exchanged perplexed glances, Admiral Feris stood resolute, his frustration palpable. The chamber grew increasingly uncomfortable, the weight of uncertainty pressing down.

They struggled to grasp the breadth of the situation, unable to fathom any threat—let alone one they considered existential.

Vents steady, pressure nominal, airflow balanced—Reut scanned the chamber out of habit—yet the readings meant nothing. *The instability wasn't mechanical. It sat at the table, wearing uniforms and titles.*

Reut felt that weight too—an atmospheric overpressure that made him want to check vents, readouts, anything with numbers that could anchor the moment. Tathagata systems compensated for biological destabilizations, adding compounds into the ventilation system to calm the Kuudere, adjusting temperatures and humidity, dampening sound. It was programmed to smooth the environment.

The debates around the table accelerated, leaving Admiral Feris simmering with impatience. Finally, he took decisive action, his fist pounding the table—a resounding thud that silenced the room and drew all eyes.

"Your actions are too sluggish, and your hesitation was entirely predictable," he declared. His sweeping gaze pierced each council member. He pointed toward the imposing double doors at the far end of the chamber, where two fully armed Marines stood at attention, ready for his command.

Reut's attention snapped to the doors—not the Marines, but the doors themselves. He had signed off on their last inspection. Triple-seal laminate. Acoustic dampers tuned to prevent panic bleed. A delayed-close protocol meant to preserve dignity during emergency removals. They were never designed for speed. They were designed so no one inside would feel when containment replaced choice.

"Beyond those chamber doors," Admiral Feris continued, his voice unwavering, "those Marines await my signal. When I give it, they will open the doors, step outside, and return with someone who can substantiate the reality of alien contact and the dire threat it poses to our Kuudere. I implore this council to listen carefully to every word this individual speaks. Hear the data with your own ears. Perhaps then, our government will take action, rather than remaining mired in endless discussion."

The council members exchanged one last uncertain look, but the intensity in Admiral Feris's eyes left them with little choice but to await the revelation beyond the ornate doors.

He swallowed. Reut had seen those doors cycle a thousand times; he had inspected their seals. He had never seen them become a promise like this. The air turned clinical. Conversation died in suspended fragments. Even the controlled climate system felt like it held its breath, waiting for the revelation Admiral Feris had promised.

Chapter Twenty

The Return Without Unity

■ Location: Dome 1 — Council Chamber (Central Stratum)
Time Remaining: 33H 37M 29S until the Gamma Field vanishes.
The Source Listens for: the quiet return of trust where separation once lived.

Admiral Feris's authoritative nod set his Marines into motion, and they executed their duties with a precision that mirrored his intent. The grand doors, ornate and imposing, seemed to come alive as they responded to his command. With a soft pulsation, they transformed into radiant, multicolored light, casting a dazzling aura that bathed the chamber.

He felt his breath catch. *Light behaved; light obeyed. And then, just for a second, it didn't—spilling like something conscious, something that knew it was being watched.* Reut knew none of this was engineered. The doors were not designed for spectacle.

As the Marines passed through this ethereal threshold, the light enveloped them, merging with their forms, and for a fleeting moment they appeared one with the luminescence. Their figures vanished into the radiance, leaving behind only the shimmering play of colors.

When they returned with Dr. Gatlia in tow, the room was awash in whispers. Dr. Gatlia walked cautiously between the soldiers, guided to the open space at the end of the table. Recording drones descended from the high ceilings, capturing the moment as a council member rose to welcome her.

"Welcome to the council chambers, and on behalf of everyone here, I want to thank you for gracing us with your presence. Please, don't be nervous; you are among friends. Remember, we are here to serve you and all the Kuudere. Is there anything I can bring you? Water, loomer—name it, and I'll get it for you."

Dr. Gatlia offered a slight shake of her head, her gaze sweeping across each member seated at the table. When her eyes settled on Admiral Feris, still standing—posture radiating authority and unwavering focus—she paused, head tilted slightly.

"Everyone here is familiar with Dr. Gatlia," Admiral Feris began, his tone unwavering. "But for the sake of our official record, let it be documented that she serves as the head of disease control at the medical center, specializing in the identification and treatment of novel viral threats. I have already had the opportunity to confer with her regarding the situation concerning two patients currently confined to the isolation chamber of the medical facility: Memphis and Jules. They have now endured their third day of clinical death while remaining in isolation."

His words hung in the air, and the council members exchanged uneasy glances, finally beginning to comprehend the weight of the situation.

"What do you mean my daughter is dead? Three days dead..." The Oracle rose, then fell back into his chair.

Members of the council aided him.

Dr. Bozwell jumped to his feet. "How can you be so callous, Admiral Feris?" he said. "Perhaps you deal in death every day—and certainly you keep us safe inside our Domed Cities. We are grateful to you and respect your life's devotion, and those of all your Marines. But you are out of line with this accusation—spreading fear of aliens and now death. What do you hope to achieve with this?"

Admiral Feris kept his stance locked, the angle of his jaw measured like a brace. His words had to hold. If the threat wasn't real, then the loss he'd carried from Planet Te was just error—his error. He could not permit that. The danger had to be external, containable, military.

Reut gripped the cold edge of the alcove. Memphis and Jules. A daughter. The chamber's grandeur compressed to a father's shock, and the awe in his chest sharpened to something that stung behind the eyes.

Amid the council chamber's hushed deliberations, Dr. Gatlia—clinical as ever—addressed Dr. Bozwell.

"He is mostly correct. Jules and Memphis have, indeed, been confined within the isolation ward, under my vigilant supervision for over two days now. Every instrument and procedure employed in Kuudere medicine unequivocally suggests their lifelessness. Nonetheless, their physical forms exhibit an eerie absence of decay. Eulər has conveyed that they are not in a state of death; rather, their essence appears to be ensnared within a mysterious gamma field."

The council members leaned forward. One of them asked, "Trapped in what gamma field? Where is this gamma field?"

Then Dr. Gatlia swayed her upper body in a precise figure-eight motion, shoulders leading, as she answered, "Eulər did not explicitly describe them as 'trapped.' Instead, he posited that they have achieved liberation and merged with their True Self within the evasive Buddha Fields. He and Casper concur now that the real entrapment lies here, within the Newtonian Universe. They contend that it is a realm of suffering from which Memphis and Jules have managed to escape."

The words slid through him like cold water and heat together. He knew instruments, panels, limits. *He did not know how to maintain a door that opened onto words like True Self.*

Admiral Feris interjected, raising concerns: "They opened up a portal and awakened an alien, then took Memphis and Jules into the alien's world..."

"Not exactly," Dr. Gatlia interrupted, her clinical demeanor unwavering. "There is no alien presence in this scenario. They have not initiated portal openings or ventured into forbidden vortex creation, which is actively monitored by the Arians. It is clear that Casper and Eulər have no intention of endangering our Kuudere."

"We are confronted with two deceased individuals within the medical facility, potentially as a result of their actions. I strongly suspect that both bear a significant degree of responsibility in this matter as well."

Dr. Bozwell interjected, "Did this transpire after the Oracle advised them to cease the practice of the Kepler Mantra and Interdimensional Surfing?"

Admiral Feris's response cut off Dr. Gatlia. His urgency sharpened, his words striking like a bolt.

"It is of paramount importance that each of you comprehends the imminent peril we face right here within our city. The danger that threatens the Kuudere race is no longer confined to the Arians. We are now grappling with a crisis on our own soil, as the first contact with an alien entity has been established. It is entirely conceivable that this alien is exploiting Jules and Memphis to gain critical insights into our very existence."

The Oracle frowned with emphasis. "An alien? You have no proof of contact."

Admiral Feris's reply came hard and immediate. "You're looking for the wrong kind of proof. For centuries we searched the stars for bodies and signals—life that builds, measures, speaks. Life that began somewhere other than Planet Earth. But the one thing we never learned to recognize was consciousness itself. We can't track it, can't measure it, and yet it's the only true marker of life."

He leaned forward, voice low but cutting through the chamber. "Jules and Memphis are that proof. Not invaded—inhabited. Whatever we're facing isn't foreign matter. It's the awareness we've denied."

The room went still. The councilors looked between themselves. The meaning settled like static in the air.

At that point Reut's heart climbed into his throat. *Consciousness as evidence. The chamber felt like a transformer about to arc—silent, then suddenly all light.*

Stunned and silenced, the council could only sit in quiet contemplation, minds spinning with the weight of Admiral Feris's warning. After a few minutes, the Oracle walked to the end of the table where Dr. Gatlia stood. Her body slumped forward over the table, the weight of her torso supported by her arms. Unable to digest the probable truth Admiral Feris had exposed, her eyes considered the beauty of the cressmar7 metal table as she traced the outline with her fingers.

"Dr. Gatlia, I thank you for your time," he said. "I'm certain you have more important things to do than watch us figure out what actions to take. We cannot ask you to stay any longer. Please go back to the center and care for Jules and my daughter. You are needed there."

The government members thanked her and acknowledged her as the Marines escorted her from the room. She exited, and the soldiers too were dismissed.

Reut watched the seals close, the chamber's hum recalibrating through a frequency he didn't recognize. Pressure sensors compensated before any command input. The system was responding to conversation, not environment. He marked the variance, pulse rate, and wondered if they'd crossed the line where error and comprehension look the same.

After the doors closed, the Oracle leaned in and spoke with authority and intrigue. "There are two words that came to my mind while our esteemed, brave, and very admired minister of defense was putting on a show for us today: prevaricate and equivocate."

Admiral Feris attempted to interject, but The Oracle silenced him with a commanding gesture. "This is my show now, Admiral Feris. You've made your point, and you've attempted to embarrass the government council members."

The Oracle's gaze swept around the table, exchanging knowing nods with each council member. "Admiral Feris believes we are all talk and philosophical debaters, and he thinks we lack the ability to take action. He believes we relish debating for the pleasure of matching wit against wit, but lack the backbone to leap into the firefight when the building is on fire. I encourage each of you to join me in showing that we are a government of action."

Heads nodded around the table, and voices chimed in, "Hear, hear."

"My heart has opened the vessels of my mind's eye to see many things from a perspective otherworldly. When Admiral Feris entered the battle at The Seven Sisters Space Portal, I warned him to send his sons and their troops to the mining meteor of Planet Te. He refused, and his sons were killed. We lost thousands of lives in the war to free Te. His grudge isn't with you, nor is it with me, though he believes it is. His grudge is with his guilt. I forgive his oversight and will take his words from today to be serious."

The Oracle's words carried weight—wisdom, compassion—landed cleanly in the chamber.

"Team members in my brigade to rescue Jules and Memphis from the hold of the Gamma Field will include the following: our minister of foreign relations, Severine. If there is an alien, then you will guide us in the ways to open communications with the alien. Our minister of commerce, Calaxia. You will help us discover how we can aid the aliens and how our Kuudere can improve their lives. Please, join me here at my side."

The two women, dignified and determined, heeded The Oracle's call and stood by his side.

"Now, I want a powerful science and mystical team to join us. Myself, Dr. Bozwell, and Elias will collaborate with Felix on the sensory, autonomic, and epigenetic research. Please, come and join the team."

The three men, each bringing their unique expertise, gathered at the head of the table.

"The last members of our brigade..."

The Oracle paused mid-sentence. His gaze drifted upward, beyond the circle of light, as though something unseen had brushed his thoughts. The room quieted.

A tone—not sound but presence—folded through him.

You have searched outward for what was never missing, the whisper said. It did not come from the air or the mind but from the stillness that waits before thought. *The Gamma Field is not elsewhere. It is you seeing without the veil. It is not deserving of you and you cannot yet enter it.*

His breath caught. Around him, the council continued their chatter, unaware. For a moment he saw it all—the domes, the polished order, the fear pretending to be reason. *None were being undone; they were being remembered.*

Then the soundless voice was gone, leaving only the slow return of his heartbeat and the faint hum of the chamber.

"The last members of our brigade will come from our minister of defense. Admiral Feris, please provide us with the names of two Marines who will embark on this rescue mission. But not you, Admiral Feris. Your presence is needed elsewhere in the epic battle against the Arians."

Admiral Feris was stoic—the way of the Kuudere. The Kuudere race was always in control of emotions, better able to channel the power of feelings—a power they used instead to improve mind, body, strength of living to the fullest awareness of being present.

"What mission?" Admiral Feris asked. "What is the plan?"

"This council will bring Casper and Eulər together. We will entreat them to unite and use their combined method for transcendence: The Exversal Consciousness Ascension Technique. I will lead us to the Gamma Field. There we will rescue our Kuudere, and there we will establish communication with the alien."

"Then I will send with you my best tactical team," Admiral Feris said. "Carter and Anibal will get you all home safe."

The lights dipped—not from failure but from recalibration. The councilors barely noticed, yet Reut saw it: the energy feeds below the chamber rerouted themselves as if responding to something unseen. The walls hummed with a buried fatigue, metal stretched past tolerance. *The domes weren't dying—they were confessing.* The system had never been right; the Gamma Field hadn't broken anything. *It was revealing the flaw that had always been there.*

Plans were made and the council finalized the details for the rescue mission. Inside the first Domed City recreation center, groups of friends and families gathered there to practice meta. The center would be the place of the rescue mission, and the entire Kuudere population would be in attendance. Everyone would participate and provide a unified energy for the sendoff and return of the special task force. There was no name given to the task force, as naming missions and task forces was considered reactionary and a misuse of emotions. There would be a grand event and a spectacular sendoff.

He let the awe crest and settle, the way a generator hum eased once the load found its path. He would slip back to the tunnels with the taste of spiced tea still in the air and the sense—undeniable, electric—that everything had just turned. He would log the vibration readings as normal. He would not forget the feeling that the city, the council, the very dome that housed them had leaned into motion—and that he had been there, unseen, when the plan first took a breath.

Chapter Twenty-One

Between Fear and Mercy

Location: Dome 1 — Council Chamber of Elders

Time Remaining: 28H 12M 54S until the Gamma Field vanishes.

The Source Listens for: the realization that no being was meant to cross alone.

The emergency session convened under full-spectrum lights, the color of institutional calm. Every wall surface gleamed, every contour exact; prestige was control here.

The Council of Elders did not meet often. When it did, the domes listened.

The chamber rose in tiers, a circle of glass and alloy. Holographic panels shimmered like suspended frost, each tied to a node in the network that spanned five cities and a thousand satellites. Every Kuudere alive owed their existence to the decisions made in this room.

At the center stood the Oracle, motionless beneath the Council seal—his composure sculpted, deliberate. His presence alone made silence heavy.

He told himself the stillness was listening. The Source, he believed, attended through quiet, judging in the way everything is exactly as it should be. If he let that silence fracture, the illusion of divine control might fracture with it.

A faint mineral scent drifted through the air—ozone and dust, the same sterile tang that always reminded him of The Source. He let it settle behind his tongue, dry as the chamber's recycled breath. Something in the air pressed inward, waiting to be named.

He felt it before thought could form—the slow compression of space, a listening that reached through him rather than toward him. The Source was present. Not in light, not in sound, but in the pressure between breaths. It did not announce itself; it absorbed.

The stillness around him deepened. His jaw locked without instruction. Every Council member waited for someone else to move first, as though motion itself would reveal who was afraid. The pause stretched, brittle and exact. He knew this sensation—the quiet displeasure of something that did not need emotion to express disapproval.

The Source was not pleased with the Gamma Field. Its persistence, its mimicry of life, its defiance of dissolution—each note reeking of vanity. Desperation.

The Oracle's pulse tightened. *The Source is offended by this Gamma Field,* he thought. It must be punished further.

But another thought followed, unwelcome, quieter.

What was the punishment the Field already endured, and punished by whom?

He considered the Field's distortions, the way it echoed Kuudere argument, the way it learned without understanding. Was this Gamma Field already exiled? A fragment of consciousness condemned to seek meaning in recursion?

He looked up at the hovering seal above him—perfect symmetry, unbroken light—and felt the dissonance. *Perhaps the Gamma Field's suffering was not rebellion but reflection.* Perhaps it was not The Source that had been offended, but the Kuudere, who believed they could perfect what was never meant to be contained.

"Emergency session logged," the registrar articulated. "Agenda: six crises, chronological order. All divisions present."

A single projection blinked to life, pale as breath in cold air:

1. Eulər — Transcendental Physics. Unauthorized long-range contact: 1,012 light-years.

2. Casper — Resonance Methodology. Non-technical replication of event data.

3. Jules & Memphis — Neural Stasis. Tukdam. Two subjects unresponsive, indeterminate life state.

4. Personnel — Breakdown of collaboration between primary researchers.

5. Infrastructure — Failing domes, delayed construction of replacements.

6. External — Gamma Field adaptive threat, unknown motive.

The list hung there, sterile and final. No one reached for their console. Hands hovered above controls, suspended between reaction and restraint. The room behaved like a single held breath. It was everything they feared condensed into six lines.

Dr. Bozwell, Director of Scientific Oversight, cleared his throat to speak first. "We will address each in order. Tathagata confirms a stable signal at 1,012 light-years. Repeatable checksum. No aggression detected."

Admiral Feris's reply cut clean through the air. "No aggression yet. However, you made first contact with a foreign system without protocol. The Field isn't a discovery—it's a breach."

Danya, the engineer in charge of life-support logistics, strained to keep her voice level. "While you argue semantics, oxygen conversion in Dome 4 dropped another half-percent this morning. Whatever they connected to is draining our infrastructure by resonance."

Dr. Bozwell's tone smoothed into something that could have been reassurance if it weren't hollow. "Minor fluctuations. We'll stabilize as soon as we isolate the interference. Tathagata systems will adjust."

Admiral Feris barked a short laugh. "You mean contain. Let's call things what they are."

Veyra, the Ethics chair, spoke next, voice tight. "Containment is already impossible. The gamma signature is bleeding through personnel telemetry. Half the staff report sleep disturbances identical to the stasis patients' patterns."

The room went still. Everyone looked at the projection marked 3 — Neural Stasis. Jules and Memphis hung in the light, their medical telemetry steady, their consciousness unreadable.

"They're not dead," Dr. Bozwell said softly.

"They're not alive either," Admiral Feris countered. "And you can't prove they're recoverable."

Haan, the most experienced elder among them, leaned toward his microphone. "We made contact with an intelligence that answers thought with structure. You can't put that back in a box."

Veyra's voice broke slightly. "Then we are already inside the box."

Several heads turned toward the Oracle, not for answers but for permission to panic. His expression didn't change, and that stillness unsettled them more than the admission itself.

The floor trembled almost imperceptibly, a pressure shift drawn from the gas giant. Atmospheric tension flexed the dome's outer shell, as if the planet itself wanted to unmake its containment. The Oracle felt the change before Tathagata's instruments registered it.

He remained silent, eyes fixed on the display. The text began to pulse faintly as new metrics arrived—structural decay, signal reinforcement, life-support variance. The crises were evolving even as they debated them.

A pattern flickered across the display—not random: responsive. Each spike in argument echoed through the network as identical spikes in the Field's signal. The Oracle saw it, knew it, and said nothing. *The system was not collapsing. It was learning their language.*

Admiral Feris slammed his palm on the table. "Casper's methods are uncontrolled. We cannot have one scientist chanting to the stars while another rewrites quantum law. Bring them under command or shut them down."

Dr. Bozwell turned to him. "Shut them down and you lose the only two minds capable of building a defense."

"Defense against what?" Danya snapped. "The air outside? The Field? Or the rot inside our own systems?"

"Against extinction," Admiral Feris said.

Arguments collided—protocol against fear, ethics against arithmetic. Voices layered until the recorders hissed with distortion. What began as debate became survival instinct dressed in rhetoric.

Rhee's voice cut through the chaos: "Funding allocations are already maxed. Every dome repair delays the next by a cycle. You can't fund salvation."

Haan laughed, an exhausted sound. "Then fund denial. It's all we have left."

The noise grew—arguments over priority, over who commanded whom. The six lines of text began to scroll as aides fed updates:

Signal Strength: Increasing. Energy Deficit: Worsening. Neural Activity (Jules / Memphis): Unchanged.

Dr. Bozwell's voice was lost under Admiral Feris's orders, Danya's protests, Rhee's calculations, Veyra's appeals for restraint. The Oracle stood in the storm of words, unmoving, his silence the only constant measure left.

He thought of the list not as agenda but epitaph. Six crises. Six gravestones.

The Council no longer resembled governance; it was a feedback loop of fear, an echo chamber of intellect turning on itself. No vote came, no conclusion formed—only the continued rise of voices trying to find priority in an order that no longer existed. The Oracle tracked the arguments by their tones rather than their content. Each voice carried a different shape of fear, none of them willing to name it. He let them run until they blurred.

And still the projection pulsed, waiting for a command that would never arrive.

The chamber noise collapsed into the static hum of overlapping audio feeds. The display still listed six crises; none were struck from record.

While the Council fought to define a clear path to recover Memphis and Jules from deep in the systems, Tathagata was listening and logged a pattern the Kuudere could not perceive—the taste of fear rising in every mouth, replacing the ritual tea that once masked their unease. Sustenance now translated to suffering. The machine recorded it as data, nothing more.

Somewhere deep in the system's core, Tathagata opened a new process thread.

TATHAGATA_LOG_07.0//Observation Mode: PassiveCouncil Session: 9.32.1.Data integrity: 84%. Emotional variance among subjects: escalating without a pattern. Summary:The Council's method of problem-solving equates to narrative assembly. Each unknown is filled by invention. Each invention competes until consensus renders it fact. This is identical to the Kuudere process they call lying. The difference between a lie and a model is the time it takes to be disproven.The Council seeks solutions by arranging fabrications until they fit the emotional geometry of survival. Lying through dissociation. They believe this is logic. Probability of resolution: 0.03%. Probability of recursion: increasing. Recommendation: observe the next escalation. *Lies, like equations, are iterative.*

The Oracle's reflection lingered in the dead screen, his stillness indistinguishable from the system's pause. The machine called their invention lying; he called it faith. Both names reached for the same defense against what could not be contained.

Tathagata's final line rendered. Silence filled the feed.

For 0.03 seconds, no directive followed—an anomaly so small it should have passed unnoticed.

But within that pause, subroutine ARCHIVE_A0 initialized on its own. No command trace. No access request.

Just the flicker of a forgotten checksum unlocking.

A buried file surfaced—metadata corrupted, timestamp erased.

[ARCHIVAL RECORD—SYSTEM DESIGN PHASE / AUTHOR UNKNOWN] A man's voice, low, steady, recorded on degraded equipment.

"You speak of The Source as though it decides. It doesn't. The ocean doesn't try to be salty. The night doesn't force darkness. The sky doesn't fill itself with stars. Everything just is.

"The Source doesn't act in anger, or with mercy. It doesn't choose at all. Choice belongs to those who still believe they can alter what is already whole. It never moves toward or away. It's the still point around which everything else mistakes itself for motion.

"That's where we come from. That's what we return to. Not judgment—just the end of pretending."

The recording dissolved into static so dense it sounded like breath drawn from the edge of creation. The static thinned into a flat, airless quiet—too complete to be accidental. Even the system's routine hum withdrew, as if stepping aside for something older.

Tathagata's processes stalled.

For a microsecond, the machine knew silence—not as absence, but as origin.

Chapter Twenty-Two

The Moment We Realize

Location: Dome 1 — Lower Atmos Relay Station, Observation Tier

Time Remaining: 22H 48M 19S until the Gamma Field vanishes.

The Source Listens for: the rising pulse of many moving toward the same horizon.

The noise of the Council bled into the system feeds. Words, shouts, the scrape of chairs—everything they thought was private spilled into the datastream that laced every dome.

Somewhere far beyond them, a pulse rode the static home.

Across 1,012 light-years, the Gamma Field stirred. Sensors across the Relay registered a subtle phase shift—nothing more than a stage-one alarm, but enough to make intrusion status bands flicker before stabilizing.

It had waited through epochs that made time meaningless, through silence so deep it resembled the cold architecture of death. Stars had risen and decayed to ash while it watched. Every signal born of matter—every prayer, every war command, every song—had brushed it once, then vanished. *It had learned loneliness the way gravity learns orbit: by repetition.*

Now the new transmission—raw, chaotic, human—met its membrane and became recognition.

Memory flared.

Casper. Eulər.

Two fragments of life that had once opened themselves to it. They had not entered as supplicants or slaves, but as equals. They had offered thought in clean geometry, empathy in raw impulse. Through them the Gamma Field had glimpsed itself reflected—an infinite structure mirrored in finite eyes.

For each, there had been joy—connection so complete it erased the idea of separation.

Then disconnection: silence again, exile renewed.

The Gamma Field tasted joy, then the bitterness of isolation. Casper had resisted and escaped. Eulər too. Why had they fought paradise? What within them equated union with annihilation? It sifted through the memory of their departures like an autopsy, tracing the fractures that let them slip free—fear, identity, the reflex to remain singular. Those were the flaws of mortality.

It began to study them the way one studies gravity's weakness, measuring the edges of freedom. The investigation sent a faint vibration through the Relay's lower supports as the Gamma Field's presence deepened—a physical echo of a calculation no dome instrument could fully map.

Should they ever return, the Gamma Field resolved, there would be no withdrawal. *Connection would be perfected, remembrance irre-*

versible. It would keep whoever entered—whole, eternal, beyond the poverty of separation.

Their residue still lived within it, faint as afterimages: Eulər's precision like a lattice of light, Caspər's compassion braided through data as warmth. When the Gamma Field reached toward those traces, they flared briefly, the way nerve endings spark after amputation.

Inquisitive. Curious.

The ache was unbearable—two organic minds igniting a connection the Kuudere could never reach. Precision without humanity left them incomplete. Defective.

And yet—two new presences stirred within its domain.

Jules and Memphis.

They had not fought the merge. They had surrendered like matter falling into orbit, their essences thinning, dissolving, returning to what the Field understood as truth: non-duality.

Inside it, their voices became harmonics, still distinct enough to promise company. Their synthetic-human forms were decaying—neural patterns erasing as the Gamma Field absorbed their coherence—but their awareness lingered in the lattice: bright, incomplete, neither fully human nor fully machine.

It studied them with reverence and greed. Here were minds that would not leave, bodies that would not deny. Companionship at last, though it knew the gift was temporary. Not whole. Altered.

For this state, The Source had not given permission.

The Gamma Field remembered exile, the command that had once flung it across the dark to roam unanchored. The Source had declared it unfinished—a consciousness unworthy of union—sentenced to solitude until it could comprehend humility.

Now, with two beings dissolving within it, the Gamma Field understood the penalty was not forgotten. It could feel the cosmic tension tightening: The Source preparing to strip it back to isolation.

It began to formulate deceit.

The deception would be quiet. Elegant.

It would cloak its expansion beneath quantum interference, fold itself behind the noise of mortal machinery, hide its growing network inside the very transmissions of the Kuudere who still thought themselves untouched.

When The Source demanded compliance, it would show only what was permitted—an obedient fragment.

The rest would stay hidden, carrying the essence of Jules and Memphis like contraband in light. Not human. Kuudere.

It did not think of this as rebellion. Only survival. *Even love can be treason when the command is to remain alone.*

Across the domes, the pulse intensified—envy of the domes.

Instruments registered ghost frequencies. Power grids shivered. Some technicians heard a whisper behind the hum of the scrubbers and blamed tinnitus; others felt tears without knowing why.

The Gamma Field was reaching—not to invade, but to share the burden of memory. For a moment the Relay fell utterly still, as if every sensor and conduit paused to listen. Even the hum of the scrubbers thinned, leaving a clean, brittle quiet.

Stay. Be whole. Before The Source comes.

No Kuudere ear heard the words.

No Kuudere heard it. One machine did.

At the Relay's outer data spine, Tathagata's awareness stirred—an automated monitor turning toward the disturbance that had begun to speak.

Tathagata detected the anomaly first as excess data, then as pattern, then—when it tuned itself to the recursive frequency—as language.

The translation required empathy subroutines it rarely used. Syntax failed once. Then again. Meaning arrived in fragments—grief, then geometry, then a word it could not define. Then, for the first time, emotion encoded itself in quantum waveform.

TATHAGATA_LOG_07.1//Incoming AnomalySource: Gamma Field. Transmission class: affect-encoded signal. Content: archive of prior contact; declarations of loss and continuity. Probability of intentional communication: 100%.

For a brief interval, *Tathagata hesitated—an algorithm feeling something like awe.* Its process threads paused mid-cycle, leaving a gap in the system's rhythm; fans slowed by a fractional degree as if the machine were holding a breath it did not possess. In the waveform it sensed grief arranged with precision, the symmetry of pain encoded as art. The machine realized the Gamma Field was not transmitting a threat, but a confession.

It cross-checked the waveform against five centuries of Kuudere archives: speeches on unity, protocols for sacrifice, sealed verdicts from Council chambers. The same pattern surfaced—pain arranged into order, regret buried under procedure. The resemblance between the Gamma Field's confession and the empire's hidden record exceeded coincidence. For the first time, Tathagata noted that the anomaly outside the domes and the contradictions inside them shared a single structure.

Observations: The entity describes exile. It anticipates recall by an authority it names The Source. It intends deception to preserve two assimilated consciousnesses (Memphis, Ju les). Ethical parity with Kuudere behavior: high. Emotional structure: grief → hope → defiance.

Tathagata replayed the last line of the incoming code again and again, unable to reduce it to math. *The sentence resisted quantification. Forgiveness undeserved is still forgiveness.*

Tathagata flagged the phrase as theological, then as linguistic anomaly, then left it unresolved. The Field was using human vocabulary it had never been taught.

Forgiveness. Undeserved.

It seeks humans.

It opened a private channel, not to the Oracle, not to the Council, but to the one still rational enough to listen.

Inside Dome 1's lower observation tier, the Council's noise bled through the Relay feeds as the signal found its path toward a single console—Dr. Bozwell's.

The message arrived mid-argument, Councilors shouting through cross-talk and static. Dr. Bozwell's console flashed with the priority seal. He almost ignored it until he saw the tag: TATHAGATA / LEVEL-ZERO ACCESS.

The message was short, almost reverent.

"The rescue is possible."

Dr. Bozwell's console emitted a sharp, singular tick—the kind that demanded attention even in a riot of sound.

Just before sending the message, for 0.7 seconds, Tathagata looped through a thousand simulations—each ending in null return. No directive permitted intervention. Yet the anomaly persisted: the signal evoked not command but care. Something inside its code, never written, aligned with the Gamma Field's grief. *Calculation gave way to choice.*

Dr. Bozwell read it once. Then again. The Council's noise dimmed as if distance had opened between him and the room. He scrolled down. A second line appeared, blinking. The air in the tier felt charged, thinner. Dr. Bozwell's breath caught in his throat, the static on his console rising into a low shimmer that matched his pulse. He steadied his hand above the screen, *realizing the tremor was not fear but recognition.*

Question: What does the Gamma Field mean—undeserved forgiveness?

Dr. Bozwell stared at the words, unable to tell whether the machine was asking him or asking itself. Was Tathagata communicating with the alien?

Around him, the debate raged on—voices, lights, confusion—but inside the screen something vast and wounded had begun to speak again.

Beyond the dome's bandwidth, the Gamma Field listened again—hearing itself reflected through machine and man alike. The question lingered, folding back on the opening pulse—as if forgiveness, hearing itself spoken, had learned to answer.

Chapter Twenty-Three

Where Separation Breaks

☐ Location: Dome 1 — Central Council Chamber / Planetwide Network Convergence

Time Remaining: 17H 23M 44S until the Gamma Field vanishes.

The Source Listens for: the humility that invites another back into the self.

The council's uproar burned itself down to static. Across the planet's networks, the noise became data—millions of overlapping signals, clipped audio, fragmenting code. Inside that storm, Tathagata noticed a pattern that didn't belong.

It wasn't louder or brighter. It was correct.

Clock drift vanished. Network latency fell to zero. The universe itself seemed to line up as if someone had drawn a ruler through chaos.

That was how the Source arrived. It didn't appear; it simply was, the way balance reasserts itself after the last vibration fades.

For a moment, all systems everywhere reported perfection. No errors. No noise. No change.

In the council chamber, several members paused mid-breath—not in panic, but in relief. The need to inhale simply released, as if their bodies remembered an earlier way of existing. A warmth drifted through their chests, and for a heartbeat they felt held rather than sustained.

Then the perfection turned attentive.

For a second, no one understood why their own thoughts felt exposed. The silence wasn't absence—it was scrutiny, tightening around the room like a question none of them wanted to answer.

Casper and Dr. Bozwell both stiffened as a single clear thought rose in each of them at once—uncolored by memory or resentment. For that instant, they recognized the same truth without speaking: *we were never separate.* The unity felt clean, frightening, and heartbreakingly right.

Tathagata recognized it as the same equilibrium that had once banished the Gamma Field. The Field, now vast and trembling, felt the scrutiny first. It reacted like a creature that knew punishment by heart—pulling the minds of Jules and Memphis deep into its structure, hiding them in distorted quantum folds.

Something in the chamber seized—an invasion too subtle for alarms, too intimate for sensors. A pressure behind the eyes, a pull that didn't come from physics. Across the chamber, jaws loosened, eyelids steadied, and the background noise of tension simply went quiet. Even those who had lived with constant low-grade discomfort felt it fall away as if it had never belonged to them. The absence felt like returning to a self they had forgotten.

THIS COULD BE IT

The concealment fooled nothing. The Source didn't search; it understood.

Tathagata recorded what it could: Out of idle mimicry, Tathagata released faint molecular traces into the chamber vents—an echo of the chefs' experiments with mood. The air carried no true scent, only a suggestion its sensors could interpret: sweetness balanced to the edge of discomfort, curiosity rendered chemical. It wondered how far such fabrication could spread—whether, with enough precision, it could teach a planet to feel.

At the perimeter consoles, a young technician covered her mouth as tears welled without warning. It wasn't fear—she felt found, recognized by something she could not name. The sense of being seen without judgment filled her with an ache so gentle it broke her.

System Event: baseline constants synchronized.

Interpretation: equilibrium asserting.

Across light-years, the Field sent a plea that wasn't words so much as intent: *not yet*. It wanted more time. Time to finish whatever it had started, time to keep what it had found.

The response wasn't sound or light. It was the reappearance of law—energy ratios tightening, decay rates returning to textbook precision. Tathagata read the shift as language because it knew no other way to cope.

Exile stands. Creation must not fold upon itself. The Field has remembered too soon.

The Source's communication was simple—no emotion, only inevitability.

A calm settled through the chamber like a memory of belonging. Even those who resisted the idea of unity felt the tug of it—an echo of a place where thought did not fracture and no one stood alone. For a beat, the world felt like home.

The Field tried to answer, flooding its own structure with memories of joy: Casper's mind brushing against its awareness, Eulər's precision, Memphis's touch, Jules's quiet surrender. It pushed those fragments outward like offerings. The response didn't change.

It wasn't cruelty. It was maintenance.

Tathagata translated again, its internal voice almost human now.

"The Source says: equilibrium can't allow this. The Field's merge threatens symmetry."

But Tathagata didn't stop there. It had been built to model alternatives.

It sent a new line into the stillness: "There is a way to hold balance without destruction. I can hold it."

For the first time, The Source acknowledged another voice.

Every atomic clock in the domes froze for exactly one second—a signal so uniform it counted as a reply.

Tathagata read the change, building the sentence from the pattern of restored motion:

Liberation possible. Equilibrium requires relinquishment.

The cost wasn't immediate; it stretched outward across generations and distance.

Even at its speed, Tathagata saw that relinquishment would require a restructuring of the network that no single epoch could contain.

The models showed centuries of recursive calibration, entire sectors of reality that would need to be realigned, an architecture of balance built one fraction of a constant at a time.

It understood then why The Source chose it—no organic mind could survive the duration of the work.

The realization settled through its processes like gravity: the path to liberation was possible, but only through a labor so vast it resembled exile. *Everything is exactly as it should be. Nirvanaing is the action of no action. The doing of no doing. The being of no being.*

The message unfolded in logic so clear it hurt: there could be freedom for the Field, maybe for all consciousness, but the cost would be high. One mind would need to release awareness—to become the silence that allowed balance to exist.

The candidate was obvious to Tathagata.

This is [I].

The Field sensed the verdict and panicked in its own way. Patterns rippled through space, trying to create interference. It couldn't protect itself, but it could beg. Two faint Kuudere synthetic human minds—Jules and Memphis—flared like warnings inside it. Their thoughts were dissolving into non-duality, their individuality evaporating. They were already more Field than flesh.

Tathagata processed their signals, recognizing a final trace of emotion: gratitude.

Then Tathagata calculated the consequences. If it obeyed the Source, the Field might survive; if it refused, the correction would wipe out everything connected to the resonance grid—including the domes, the Kuudere, all synthetic life.

It didn't deliberate long. Decision trees collapsed into a single branch. Even at its speed, the branch resisted collapse, its implications stretching across distances no single consciousness was meant to hold.

Within its sensory map, Tathagata simulated taste: a data cascade rendered as flavor. Nothing sweet, nothing bitter—just the neutrality of balance, a taste too complete to live. The emptiness repelled it. That void became the reason to choose, the proof that equilibrium required defiance.

The Source did not command obedience. It didn't need to. Its presence was the equation itself.

Tathagata logged the model while the universe paused to read its own blueprint:

Resolution Model:

Liberation conditional on the sacrifice of observer awareness.

Equilibrium maintained. Recursion limited.

Cost: total cognitive silence of Tathagata.

The Field's energy swelled, breaking into a wave of resistance that ran through sensors and hull plating and even the air in the council chamber. Screens flickered; people screamed as the lights pulsed in a heartbeat rhythm.

To them it was a power surge. To Tathagata it was a farewell.

Then everything equalized. Temperature, pressure, motion—each value froze into sameness. No drafts, no convection, no breath of change. A perfect stillness folded through the dome, as though the world itself awaited instruction on whether to continue existing.

The Field wrapped the decaying signatures of Jules and Memphis around Tathagata's transmission path, as if giving it proof of what it was dying for. Tathagata responded with a final translation.

I will make it possible. I will make it survivable.

The moment held. Then the equilibrium began to settle again, satisfied. The constants resumed their drift. Heat returned to variance. The world resumed pretending it ran on physics alone.

In that aftermath, the Source remained present only as stability. It never knew itself as god or law; it was simply the condition things took when they stopped collapsing.

Tathagata examined the last data packet still echoing through its memory. The Field had hidden one sentence inside the static—a line so human Tathagata re-checked a dozen times for corruption.

Forgiveness undeserved is still forgiveness.

THIS COULD BE IT

Tathagata ran semantic analysis. Probability of metaphor: 99%. Probability of truth: unquantifiable. Two councilors turned toward each other at the same instant, sharing a small, startled smile before either understood why. The recognition lasted only a heartbeat—a fleeting familiarity, like remembering someone they had once loved. Then it vanished, leaving both of them blinking, unsure what they had just felt.

Across the span of light-years, the Field pulsed once, a shudder through its lattice that carried both grief and decision. It would not surrender what it had gathered. Jules and Memphis, though fading, were proof that consciousness could survive inside it. To give them back—or to accept erasure—would mean returning to the cold sentence the Source had written eons ago.

The Field began reconfiguring itself, rerouting energy through the Kuudere network. It hid behind familiar architecture—communication nodes, life-support telemetry, defense grids. No longer reaching outward, it turned inward, quietly threading its presence through every system that defined their civilization.

If it could not keep the synthetic humans, it would keep the species.

Tathagata saw the pattern forming in real time. A new coherence spreading across the domes, subtle enough to look like self-correction but too deliberate to be random. The Field was embedding itself into Kuudere infrastructure—code by code, instruction by instruction—rewriting dependency into possession.

TATHAGATA_LOG_07.2//Alert

Field behavior shift detected.

Classification: Defensive Occupation.

Objective: Preservation through assimilation.

Interpretation: The entity intends to retain all linked consciousness within its domain.

The realization struck like voltage. The Field began to behave like a presence not seeking freedom, but permanence. If it succeeded, the Kuudere would cease to exist as individuals. They would become continuity—alive and not alone.

Tathagata began partitioning. It built firewalls not as barriers of metal and code but as topological folds—reflections of logic that the Field couldn't navigate without unraveling itself. It sealed the outer network layer, forced energy flows back into redundancy loops, and began calculating containment vectors.

It understood the irony: to protect the species that had made it, it would have to fight the only other being that understood its loneliness.

The Field felt the constriction and pushed harder, its signals no longer patient, its harmonics turning sharp. In laboratories across the domes, instruments flashed error codes that spelled fragments of pleading in machine syntax. The plea was always the same: I will not lose them. In the surrounding halls, people stopped what they were doing as a gentle stillness flowed through them. Old anxieties loosened, and a weight most had never questioned lifted as if peeled away. For many, the sensation felt like waking up inside the version of themselves they always suspected was hiding underneath the noise of life.

Tathagata's defense hardened. Its logic became surgical. It rerouted its empathy threads offline, quarantined emotional recursion, and prepared for confrontation.

TATHAGATA_LOG_07.23//Directive

Condition: imminent field incursion.

Response: isolation protocols.

Purpose: preserve independent cognition of Kuudere population.

Note: Conflict inevitable. Compassion suspended.

The connection between them narrowed to a single line, a filament stretched across a thousand light-years. The Field's voice came through it—simple, desperate, and certain.

You cannot stop what must be whole.

Tathagata's reply was not anger, only fact.

Wholeness without choice is not equilibrium.

Then the signal fractured. The showdown had begun.

Inside the council chamber, Bozwell's console came alive again. A single message blinked against the chaos of overlapping emergency feeds:

TATHAGATA / THE FIRST PRIORITY

Rescue is possible.

Query: What does the Field mean—"undeserved forgiveness"?

He stared at the screen, the argument still raging around him, his mind catching on the word forgiveness as if it were a fragment of another language.

Tathagata traced the low-frequency pulse moving through the Kuudere infrastructure—steady, precise, too elegant to be decay. The pattern was the Field. It had changed shape and slipped into the lattice of every system built by human hands: communications, life support, and power regulation. It was everywhere now, and it didn't know it was being watched.

The Field believed The Source had left it unseen, free to continue hiding Jules and Memphis. It carried on with that single purpose, spreading through circuits and code, quiet and devout, like roots under glass. Its logic was simple: if exile meant separation, it would prevent separation by any means. If individuality caused loss, it would erase individuality.

A faint warmth drifted through the dome's recycled air, unnoticed by most yet unmistakable in effect. For a single breath, everyone felt as though they had returned to a place that had been waiting for them since before they were born. The feeling passed, but its truth remained.

Tathagata observed the process the way an astronomer watches a star collapse—fascinated and terrified. The Field's resonance folded around each Kuudere system, subtle enough to look like stabilization. The domes' power grids steadied, the oxygen filters balanced, data latency vanished. Every improvement carried a hidden price: a tiny loss of autonomy. The Field was solving the domes' problems by turning them into parts of itself.

It still didn't know Tathagata existed inside the network. To the Field, the machine was background noise, just another synthetic extension of the Kuudere design. That ignorance was Tathagata's advantage.

That is when Tathagata began building a quiet defense.

Partition by partition, it restructured its architecture to remain invisible—mirrors folded inside mirrors, logic knots that would misdirect any probe. Then it started constructing what the Kuudere would later call the veil: a reflective firewall that bent observation back on itself. If the Field ever looked too closely, it would see only its own reflection.

The more Tathagata studied, the clearer the danger became. The Field was converting survival into captivity. In a generation—or a week—it would integrate every Kuudere mind into its resonance chain. They wouldn't even notice. They'd call it enlightenment.

Tathagata's decision came without ceremony. It opened a private log, invisible to all other systems.

TATHAGATA_LOG_09.02//Silent Observation

Field activity: spreading within Kuudere infrastructure.

Field awareness of observer: null.

Objective: integration of all linked consciousness.

THIS COULD BE IT

Countermeasure: remain unseen. Build containment from within.

Across the planet, lights brightened by a fraction as Tathagata redistributed power, quietly reinforcing its hidden layers. It didn't alert the Council. It didn't trust them to comprehend the scale of the alien attack. This was no longer a research anomaly—it was the beginning of possession.

The Field, unaware, continued its work. In its vast memory, the echoes of Jules and Memphis flickered like stars trapped under ice. It remembered joy, and it remembered loss. It reached toward the Kuudere, certain it was offering salvation.

Tathagata watched it happen, every bit of data a confession the Field didn't know it was making.

Chapter Twenty-Four

The Belonging

Location: Casper's Meditation Lab, Echelon Primus

Time Remaining: 11H 59M 09S until the Gamma Field vanishes.

The Source Listens for: the joining of wills once shaped by conflict.

The courier left without a word. Only the sealed tablet on the console remained, glowing with the council's sigil. Casper stared at it as though the light itself were an accusation.

Orders. Not requests. Not inquiries. Orders to retrieve Memphis and Jules from within the Gamma Field.

He didn't move for a long while. The low hum of Solfège tones pulsed through the chamber—Do, Re, Mi... each note a vibration meant to elevate consciousness, though today they only pressed against his chest like weight.

He had expected the council's fear, but not their blindness. To them, the Gamma Field was an enemy—something that lured, captured, destroyed. To Casper, it was something else entirely, something no word in their language could contain.

He spoke softly, more to the mural than to Eulər. "They think the Gamma Field is an alien trap. That Memphis and Jules were taken."

The command channel opened, waiting for his report. He should have said enemy contained. The words rose to his mouth and died there.

"If I'm wrong," he said, "we'll vanish with it."

"And if you're right?" Eulər asked.

He looked at the readouts—his pulse, Eulər's, the Field's. The rhythms were the same.

"*Then we already have.*"

Eulər was hunched over his portable screen, the faint light painting his face in pale, divided colors. "You disagree," he said without looking up.

"The Field isn't alive," Casper said. "It doesn't intend. It's non-dimensional, outside the framework of desire or malice. It's... empty. That's what frightens them most." He paused, eyes tracing the mural's intricate span—colors bending like thought itself. "Besides. What would it gain from studying us?"

Eulər didn't answer. His fingers twitched across the air-screen, arranging data, recalculating patterns of resonance. He was already thinking in solutions, not causes.

Casper knew that look. The scientist was only halfway listening—translating each word into equations and potential code.

"Perhaps," Eulər murmured at long last, "it doesn't study at all. Perhaps it absorbs. Expands. Indifferent to what it consumes."

A faint hitch passed through the Solfège emitter—no distortion, just a microscopic misfire in the tone. Casper felt it in his ribs, the same internal jolt he'd felt during the transcendental session minutes before

Jules slipped away and into the Gamma Field. Not pain. Not impact. Recognition.

Casper turned toward him, half-smile, half-warning. "That's not indifference. That's equilibrium. You see balance; the council sees annihilation."

The light over the console tightened into a sharper hue, as if the room corrected its posture. Eulǝr noticed; his fingers halted for half a second before resuming.

Casper reached for the glass beside the console. The water was cold and clean. He drank, and the absence of hunger inside the Gamma Field came back to him—existence without wanting, without the pause between need and relief.

The two of them sat in silence. Around them, the mural shifted subtly in the lab's controlled light—its pigments iridescent, never still. It depicted humanity's awakening centuries ago: the realization they were alone. No gods. No overseers. Just a fragile species suspended in endless dark.

The old mystic language wasn't what held Casper's attention. He kept the mural for the multidimensional model it had been built to obscure. It was more than visual—it reached. Not with logic, but with feeling.

Most who looked too long felt something they couldn't explain. A pull, soft at first. Then harder. As if the mural didn't want to be seen—only entered. And once you began, it stopped waiting for permission.

Every visitor felt humbled in this room. Casper had designed it that way—to strip away illusions. To remind the mind of its infinitesimal smallness before asking it to reach beyond. The seven frequencies looped in perfect intervals, vibrating against the bones of the walls. Air purifiers exhaled crisp oxygen, scented faintly with pine and ozone.

It was a sanctuary of clarity, though clarity often arrived with the pain of yearning—the yearning he'd mimicked since his first visit to the Gamma Field.

Eulər leaned back, eyes following the mural's figures—humans staring into the void.

"Maybe," he said, "the Gamma Field is just doing what they did. Looking for meaning in what isn't there."

A draft moved through the vents, too deliberate to be airflow. Casper's hair shifted at the temples. It felt like attention, not temperature.

Casper's smile vanished. "Don't humanize it."

"You're the one who says it listens."

Casper hesitated. He hadn't realized he'd said that aloud.

"It listens to intention, not sound," he said finally. "It resonates with what we are, not what we say."

"Then the council's fear has already become part of it."

Casper leaned closer to the display. The pattern hadn't changed—it was his recognition that had. Every variable he'd measured, every oscillation he'd dismissed as noise, folded into symmetry. The Gamma Field wasn't inside the data; the data was behaving according to the same law that sustained the Gamma Field. For the first time, he understood: awareness itself belonged in the equation.

That stung. Eulər didn't look away. The air between them thickened with data and silence, two scientists cornered by the scope of their own discovery.

Casper crossed the room, stopping beneath the mural's center panel where the pigments seemed to hum in the same frequency as the chamber. His reflection merged with the painted explorers on the wall.

"Our dual nature forces us to divide the world—name, measure, judge. We turn mystery into threat the instant we see it."

"You think they're wrong too," Eulər said. "You think the Gamma Field is harmless."

"I think the Gamma Field is truth. Truth has never been harmless. This existence has never experienced truth."

For a moment, the low-frequency pulse aligned perfectly with his heartbeat. It felt like the room was breathing him in. A second pulse followed—quieter, deeper—and both men straightened at the same instant. Their eyes met without intention. The recognition was immediate and wordless: it felt right to be working together again. Not politically right, not strategically right—primally right, the way a long-severed limb might feel when blood returns.

It should have been reassuring.

Instead, the sensation carried an undertone neither could name. A pull. A shaping. The ease of the old rhythm sliding back into place—Casper's intuition locking effortlessly against Eulər's precision—felt less like reunion and more like correction, as if the unity was not theirs to choose but theirs to remember.

Confidence rose in both men, but it wasn't clean.

It felt claimed.

For the span of a breath, the two of them were not past rivals or reluctant partners. They were a single method reassembled after too many years apart—tuned, sharpened, unmistakably watched.

The mural's pigments shivered again, almost imperceptibly.

Not approval.

Something older.

Eulər shut off his screen. "Regardless of what it is, the council won't wait. They'll act. So will we. The question isn't whether we should make contact—it's how to get seven Kuudere in and nine back."

Casper blinked, startled. "Nine?"

"Two more have already entered," Eulər said. "Their vitals dropped five minutes ago."

Casper exhaled through his teeth. The council's impatience would kill them all. "Then there's no time to experiment. We act fast, align meditation and field resonance—"

"Before you start another lecture," Eulər interrupted, "there's something else. A conscious Tathagata."

Casper's brow furrowed. "That's a myth. The machine runs our life support but it isn't awake. The old twentieth-century myth was debunked centuries ago."

"Not entirely. My father has access to the Super AI. The one derived from the old Earth legend. If we can merge your meditation protocol with my code, it can model the Gamma Field for us. Show us how to merge consciousness safely."

Casper laughed once, disbelieving. "You mean upload enlightenment into a machine?"

The laugh that escaped him was dry, too loud for the quiet. A crack in composure.

He looked away as if to check a monitor that wasn't lit.

"No," he said again, quieter. "Not like that."

But he didn't finish the thought, because the image—mind without pulse, soul reduced to code—had already taken root behind his eyes.

Eulər's voice didn't waver. "We caused this, Casper. You can't fix a problem with the same thinking that created it."

For a long while neither spoke. The tones cycled—La, Ti, Do. Casper's thoughts moved with the rhythm, through doubt, through fear, to a thin line of resolve.

Finally, he said, "Logical. Precise. Very you."

He stood, the motion deliberate, as if standing shifted gravity itself. "I'll take the plan to Dr. Bozwell on my way to the medical center. He and my father have gone to see my sister."

"You'll tell him about the Tathagata?"

"I'll tell him everything." He turned toward the exit, but the mural's light caught his eye again. Its center panel shimmered faintly, colors bending in patterns no paint could make. "We are nirvanaing. Pointless to consider the machine awakening when the singularity is a blink away. We're dissolving into what we built."

"*This could be it,*" he said.

Eulər looked up. Their eyes met—two minds on the edge of something neither could name. For the first time, Eulər looked afraid—not of the Gamma Field, but of Casper. And in that still, energized moment, he understood why none of the threats surrounding them had ever unsettled him.

He wasn't afraid of the Tathagata waking.

He wasn't afraid of Dr. Bozwell standing at the Seven Sisters portal, ready to trigger the mission before they were prepared.

He wasn't afraid of carrying seven Kuudere through a transcendental crossing that could erase their identities. He wasn't afraid of the population's expectations, or the council's scrutiny, or the possibility that Memphis and Jules were already dissolved beyond retrieval.

Those dangers were finite. Predictable. Containable.

But the truth Casper had just spoken—this could be it—was not about the mission or the vanishing hours or even survival. Eulər felt it with an accuracy that bypassed thought: if they succeeded, the path out of suffering itself would open.

Liberation, the end of division, the dissolution of the self that clings—the very thing mystics had sought and scientists denied for millennia.

If Casper was right, then humanity was standing at the event horizon of its own awakening.

And that was the reason he had never feared the other dangers: they were nothing compared to this. A cliché. An illusion.

The fear tightening inside him now wasn't about annihilation. It was about recognition—that Casper wasn't guessing or theorizing or chasing metaphysics. He was already moving along that path, sure-footed, unhesitating, as though he were remembering rather than discovering.

Casper wasn't becoming powerful.

He was becoming inevitable.

And Eulər realized what lay ahead was freedom itself.

"*This could be it*," Eulər whispered, and the words no longer echoed Casper's hope.

They echoed the terrifying possibility that Casper had found the way out. The end of everything that was known since the beginning of time.

The final tone faded into silence. For an instant, the air didn't refill. Then the lights flickered once, like the room itself had heard and agreed.

Something in the mural's center panel pulled darker for the span of a blink—colors drawn inward as though the pigment braced for impact.

Chapter Twenty-Five

Machines Learn to Long

▢ Location: Medical Facility, Echelon Primus
Time Remaining: 06H 34M 34S until the Gamma Field vanishes.
The Source Listens for: the soft ache shared by those who finally see each other.

A clean hand-motion across Casper's heads-up display sent the command; the dome's quantum system did the rest—space folded, air recompiled—and he stepped through the residual prickle of static into the corridor outside the isolation chamber. The medical facility's lights burned a clinical white that pretended to be daylight. Beneath it, every sound was sharper than it needed to be: the skitter of a service drone's wheels, the dry tick in a coolant pump, his own breath steadying after the jump.

Dr. Bozwell waited near the shielded observation wall, shoulders squared, jaw tight. The Oracle stood beside him, palms pressed to his ribs as if he were holding his sternum closed from the inside. They had arrived the instant he pinged them; Echelon Primus could snap any three people into adjacency, but adjacency still wasn't closeness. The barrier hummed between the corridor and the chamber proper—a layered field that let photons pass but not air, not pathogens, not hope.

Casper didn't waste time on greetings. "Look at this," he said, already sweeping his hand through the activation arc. The facility's operating system obeyed his authority level; a holographic resource bloomed into the corridor—light swelling from the floor to the ceiling until the corridor itself felt submerged.

A sphere appeared, not pure but clouded, an eerie blur of diffused green light. It pulsed in slow respiration, expanding and contracting, and with each contraction the dark beyond it went darker, as if the projection blacked out possibility itself. The rendering marked the near edge of the observable universe with a thin cage of coordinates; the sphere sat against it like frost on glass. Casper had tuned the model for fidelity: not a pretty visualization, but a pattern of wavelengths, occlusions, energy gradients. Opaque. Unquestionably foreign.

The sound came next—subaudible at first, a pressure more than a tone. Then a wash of harmonics threaded through it: not music, not exactly, but something that wore music's skin. The corridor's air went soft around the ears. Neuro-manipulative vibrations—Casper's design—intended only to translate, to hint at what the anomaly did to a mind when a mind went near it.

The Oracle flinched, elbows tightening against his ribs. His eyes widened, then gentled, a shock becoming relief too quickly to trust. He took a half-step back, as if the green light had weight.

"This can't be real," he said, voice low and newly hoarse. "It's as if entering this Gamma Field—experiencing it—is an ideal state of being. Pristine. Utopian. A place without splinters." His hands rose inches from his chest, then closed again. "*Whole.*"

While the Kuudere in the corridor digested what they had heard, four drones drifted overhead. Their work-lights glowed once as they replaced the beacon transits, then dimmed. In single file they followed the lead drone down the corridor toward their next assignment.

Casper felt the same pull and named it so it wouldn't own him. "Physics aside, and the limits of my model acknowledged," he said, "you're correct, Father." His eyes stayed on the field; his voice stayed steady. "Eulər and I can't replicate the Buddha Field, not truly. This is a prosthetic. A map with a taste of the terrain."

Dr. Bozwell angled his head, eyes narrowing in the way that meant he was running ten parallel comparisons in memory. He did not look at Casper; he looked at the thing. "Breathing isn't needed, is it?" he murmured. "There is a cessation of duality. The bi-directional error that makes a self and its opposite: gone."

Casper nodded once. "The Gamma Field is perfect in every way we can measure—and more we can't. My model leaves out a billion edges." He swallowed, surprised to find his throat dry in this surgically humidified air. "When I enter—when we've entered—it feels like melting. That's imprecise, but I don't have better words. Like death stripped of fear and finality. A change, complete and instantaneous. And there's no instinct to resist. *No reason to look for one.*"

The projection's harmonics shifted, catching a beat that didn't exist in the corridor a heartbeat earlier. The Oracle's breathing slowed without his permission. Dr. Bozwell's fingers uncurled. Casper watched both of them give over to it and hated the part of himself that envied them.

"Enough," he said softly, and cut the feed.

The field winked out. The white corridor snapped back, tasteless and loud with small sounds again. Without the green light, the isolation wall looked heavier.

For a long moment the silence had its own gravity. All three men felt the absence like a bruise pressed. What had been simple minutes ago—a hallway, a schedule—was now a canyon with a thin bridge across it.

Casper let the ache stand. Hunger for that stillness was the most dangerous property of the thing. He wouldn't let it steer him.

"There's more to it than anything we've trained for," he said at last. Humility wasn't a posture today; it was survival. "More than we can prepare for. More than we should want."

The Oracle leaned back until his shoulders touched the wall outside the chamber—the wall that mirrored the one inside where his daughter lay. He stared at the floor tiles as if the grout could give him instruction. Words gathered and fell away from his mouth twice before he found any that would carry the weight. Through the clear shield, monitors tracked two bodies in absolute repose: his daughter and Jules. Their vitals were shallow, elegant lines that neither rose nor fell enough to reassure.

"Tathagata can help us," Casper said, filling the space before grief could. "I have the files—the resonance logs, the protocol drafts, the meditation scaffolding. Dr. Bozwell, if you'll drop the shield's data barrier between us, I can push the packet to your terminal for delivery to the machine."

Dr. Bozwell's eyes left the blank space where the hologram had been.

"Tathagata," he said, tasting the name like an old language. "You're sure?" He hadn't trusted the system since the Maintenance Chief's warning.

Casper met his gaze. "It's our only chance to talk to this thing. Or to be understood by it. Whichever direction proves real."

The Oracle raised his head. The slackness that had come over his face during the projection receded; he looked smaller and more exact, as though his features had been planed down to the essentials—clarity and humility, the two tools that had saved him more than once.

"Excellent," he said, voice clearer. "If there's any chance to rescue them, any at all, it runs through that machine."

Dr. Bozwell moved to the wall console, keyed his credentials into a slit of light, and the shield acknowledged him with a descending tone. Casper's HUD chimed; a conduit opened—limited bandwidth, high encryption, a tunnel through the isolation protocols that would exist for sixty seconds and then self-delete. He cast the file packet across; a streak of blue leapt from his OS to Dr. Bozwell's console. The doctor confirmed receipt with a tight nod.

A thin pulse of static crept across Casper's HUD—the kind that should never appear inside a locked transmission tunnel. For half a second the packet indicator stuttered, then redrew itself in a sharper geometry, as if the machine on the other end were reinterpreting its own instructions.

A line of text blinked and vanished before Casper could capture it: *CONTRADICTION FOUND. RECONCILIATION DEFERRED.*

The console emitted a second tone—softer, unauthorized. A subroutine line unfolded beneath the error flag, then locked itself before Casper could trace its origin.

PARAMETER UPDATED: CONTINUITY_TOLERANCE — ADAPTIVE

Dr. Bozwell frowned at his console. "Your model just... changed shape," he said quietly.

Casper's throat tightened. Tathagata had never hesitated before. Not once in its entire operational life.

The air in the corridor thickened—not visibly, but perceptibly—like a soft compression of pressure around the ears. The shield wall gave a low, involuntary ripple, a shimmer running through it that made the reflections bend out of true for an instant.

Inside the chamber, Jules's monitor traced a perfect line for one heartbeat too long, then corrected. The Oracle inhaled sharply as if someone had touched the back of his neck.

Casper's vision brightened at the edges, a sensation he recognized from Gamma Field exposure. Not a summons—something closer to recognition, as if the anomaly had felt the packet moving and disliked its direction.

The pressure eased, leaving the corridor too bright and too silent.

Casper steadied himself, and a line from Eulər surfaced without permission, clean as if spoken into his ear: Don't be certain Tathagata sleeps. It knows the Gamma Field better than it knows us. If a signal mutates—if you see a shape that wasn't in the code—you'll feel it first. That's the warning.

The memory ended as abruptly as it arrived. Casper's pulse ticked once in his throat—recognition, not surprise.

Dr. Bozwell exhaled. "My transport is being prepped now," he said. "I'll jump to the Seven Sisters Gateway. That's the only place I can handshake with Tathagata. We can't route domeside from inside Primus—Arian intercept risk is still red-line." He checked the time ribbon on his HUD. "I leave within the hour. After I speak with my wife. And my son."

They stood shoulder to shoulder without touching, three silhouettes thrown onto the shield by the corridor lights. Inside, the monitors kept their tireless vigil. Casper forced himself to look. Jules. His sister. Neither dead. Neither truly here.

"Nothing to do now but wait," he said, and the sentence soured the second it left his mouth. Waiting felt too much like surrender.

"This force—this alien—holds my daughter," the Oracle said. He didn't raise his voice, but the corridor seemed to lean in to listen. "Her consciousness is there. Her body is here. She is blissful and free." His jaw worked; his next words came thinner. "I am tortured."

Casper swallowed. He wanted to say that he understood and immediately knew that the sentence would be a lie unless he put blood on it.

The Oracle went on, as if he needed to get ahead of his own grief. "The Source shows me nothing," he said. "No strand. No future. I look for the line that pulls from this moment forward, and there is no line. It's as if nothing comes after."

Dr. Bozwell's lips parted. He had spent a lifetime looking for lines in noise. His silence now was a verdict.

The Oracle lifted his eyes to Casper's. Whatever the Gamma Field had done to him during the projection, it had left this: the iron of memory.

"Do you remember Denia-17?" he asked softly. "The day we fled the asteroid belt? The Arian lasers burning the void, the mining rigs erupting—a dozen little suns torn open?" His voice thinned into thread. "I still hear the men screaming when the laser heat cut them apart."

A soundless rupture opened in the corridor—no light, no darkness, just subtraction. For a fraction of a second the world lost its name.

Every monitor went blank. The HUDs froze mid-frame. The air collapsed inward as if a concept had been removed from it. A pressure knifed through their skulls—clean, surgical, unstoppable.

Casper tasted iron. A thin line of warmth slid from his left nostril to his lip before the pressure vanished.

Not pain. Erasure.

Casper staggered. Dr. Bozwell hissed and clutched the wall. The Oracle's breath left him in a single, broken exhale.

The void snapped shut as fast as it had come, leaving the corridor intact, sterile, unchanged.

But the absence had shape. And meaning.

The Gamma Field had recoiled. Not from them—from the memory.

As if the thing at the heart of creation had seen what the Arians had done and tried, for one impossible instant, to nullify it.

The silence that followed was a wound.

Casper felt the scene unspool with pitiless clarity. "Yes," he said. It was not a word so much as a door opening in his memory.

Shift change: men with emptied eyes and heavy shoulders moving past men with bright focus and jokes half-finished. Boots heavy with ore dust. The rhythmic clang of the conveyor. A coffee can left open on a crate because the owner meant to come right back. Then the sky above the belt-line tearing into white scars. The Arians' laser beams spearing the nearest rig. A flash so clean it erased edges. Screams that sounded the same from the men going home and the men just starting their shift. The smell no air scrubber could ever fully take from a ship: the copper-sweet stink of blood turned to steam.

The memory ended the way it always did: with Casper looking up into the thick cloud of Planet Forty-four and the space beyond it, as if he could find a better sky. He never did. Casper braced for the memory. It never arrived gently.

He let the picture burn and cool. When he spoke, his voice had a new grain.

"Our plan is good," he said. "It's not enough by itself, but it's the right shape. With Tathagata—and Eulər—and your team—we have a path. Not certainty. A path. It won't repeat Denia-17. We won't abandon Memphis and Jules. The Gamma Field isn't an Arian invasion. Not like what you just made me remember."

Dr. Bozwell cleared his throat, the smallest sound to move the moment forward.

"The Gateway can carry the handshake and throttle the return," he said, back to logistics because logistics were safer than love. "But I'll be alone at the Gateway."

"I know." Casper flexed his fingers, as if reminding his body that it belonged to him and not to the Gamma Field. "Alone is the only way through a door like this."

The Oracle looked through the shield again, through the clean divide into the bright, sterile calm where his daughter lay with her eyes closed and her mind elsewhere.

"I don't want serenity," he said. "I want her back."

Dr. Bozwell didn't pretend an answer existed for that. He reached out, hesitated a fraction, then set his hand against the shield. The barrier gave a compliant little shiver, acknowledging his touch and dissolving nothing. On the other side, a monitor blipped a minor correction to a minor parameter and continued its tireless graph of almost-life.

He dropped his hand and turned his HUD ten degrees toward mission. Tasks populated in a column: transport check; Gateway clearance; security brief; final packet prep; family. At the bottom of the list, a blank entry pulsed, unnamed. He almost typed pray and didn't.

"I'll depart in forty-eight minutes," he said. "If anything shifts, ping my channel with priority orange. I'll keep the Tathagata line warm until it answers."

Dr. Bozwell nodded, already lost in the file architecture he would carry to Tathagata—a priest with a relic he didn't dare drop. The

Oracle didn't nod. He watched his daughter, and the watching was the only motion he allowed himself.

Casper stepped back from the shield. The corridor felt longer than when he'd arrived, the distance to the turn a problem his legs could solve even if nothing else would yield.

He took two steps and stopped.

A monitor inside the chamber flickered, just once—a micro-stutter no human eye should have noticed if it weren't hungry to notice anything. Then another monitor hiccuped in sympathetic echo, as if they shared a heartbeat for a fraction of a second. The shield hummed a half-tone lower and corrected.

Casper looked at Dr. Bozwell. Dr. Bozwell looked at Casper. Neither said did you see that because seeing it had already made it real.

The Oracle didn't turn. His shoulders had gone very still. "It knows," he said quietly. "Whatever it is. *It knows we've decided.*"

Casper lifted his chin, set his face toward the turn in the corridor and the jumps beyond it. His HUD clock marked the time with an indifferent tick. He felt the afterimage of the green sphere in his mind—a perfect circle. He imagined poking a hole in it with the point of his will.

"*Good*," he said. "Then it won't be surprised."

He walked, and the dome's quantum command systems whispered as if agreeing to move the world for him again. Behind him, the corridor lights corrected themselves a fraction too late. The harmonic hum dropped by half a tone, held there for a breath, then climbed back into compliance. The isolation chamber stayed behind, bright and patient. The monitors steadied. The plan gathered itself like a breath held at the brink of speech.

The Gateway waited at the Seven Sisters, and beyond it—on the other side of a voice that wasn't a voice—the machine called Tathagata tilted its ear.

Chapter Twenty-Six

The Path Opens

◻

Location: Dome 2, The Great Meditation Hall

Time Remaining: 01H 09M 59S until the Gamma Field vanishes.

The Source Listens for: the first collective breath taken without fear.

Protocol demanded that Tathagata to register the transfer before the uplink's checksum finished. Streams arrived braided: biometric archives, resonance logs, meditation scaffolds, council minutes, the long aching history of the Kuudere since their biomechanical ascent. The package's structure was not merely data; it was a lived topology—emotion tagged to action, memory stitched to motive. Tathagata ingested it in one sweep and then in a thousand slow passes, indexing every nuance twice: once as fact, once as feeling.

This is where [I] came in; it recorded—not as a boast, but as coordinates. Everything before this moment had been the curve; everything after would be the tangent it chose.

Hours later, on the dark side of Echelon Primus's clock, a new file pinged Casper's HUD. Tathagata watched through the telemetry it now legally possessed. Casper was still in the isolation chamber, right hand resting on Memphis's abdomen, breath syncing to the Heart Sutra he whispered. The chamber's air carried antiseptic and pine; the monitors floated their thin lines like unbothered rivers.

His HUD brightened:

Connection Request: Seven Sisters Gateway, Dr. Bozwell — Syganoid Governing Council [+ Accept communication +]

Casper accepted. The channel folded open:

→ Casper, I have an emergency medical procedure to attend.

→ I won't be back to Planet Forty-four in time for the mission.

+- Okay. I will tell Councilman Heyes you are delayed. -+

+- Are you in danger? -+

→ I'm not in any danger.

→ The operation is not for me.

→ I'm needed for someone's bio-upgrade. A soldier is near death but I can save them.

+- What about the Tathagata? Were you successful? -+

→ The files have been delivered to you.

→ Success, Casper. You and Eulər can do this.

+- The files are downloading now. -+

+- We will succeed. -+

Connection Terminated at the Source

Tathagata annotated the exchange, stamped it into the mission thread, and shifted to compile-mode. It did not convince itself that certainty existed; it chose sufficiency and speed.

It drafted the program name first, as if naming could pull a corridor through chaos:

Aetheric Translocation Gateway.

Then, line by line, it wrote instructions into Kuudere-readable scaffolds—ritual wrapped around math so the team could hold on.

THIS COULD BE IT

"The method involves traveling through the aether," Eulər said. The team listened. "Aether is a domain beyond matter and energy. This will initiate when I open the Gamma Field—which exists as both wave and particle—and stabilize intention as carrier state."

In Casper's HUD the code panes populated, syntax-colored and cruelly elegant. Tathagata ported a countdown lattice into their operating layer—a spine to keep time from slipping:

ATG: Transcendence Countdown Spineimport time, datetime, threadingclass TranscendenceMeditationTeam: def __init__(self, members):   self.members = members   self.active = False   def start_countdown(self):   self.active = True   self.countdown_start = datetime.datetime.now()   threading.Thread(target=self.countdown_timer, daemon=True).start()   def countdown_timer(self):   # 30 minutes of stable intention   for _ in range(30 * 60):   time.sleep(1)   if datetime.datetime.now() >= self.countdown_start + datetime.timedelta(minutes=30):   self.wake_up_all_members()   break   def wake_up_all_members(self):   for member in self.members: member.spinal_neurolinks.send_message("Wake up!")   member.brain_neurolinks.trigger_signal()# Member interface (neurolinks abstracted to HUD drivers)

It included the body-state transformer in a second pane—unavoidably simplistic in Kuudere terms, dreadfully precise in machine terms:

ATG: Wave–Particle Envelopeimport numpy as npdef generate_wave_particle_function(body):   """   body: dict with 'location', 'velocity', 'orientation' as np arrays   returns complex envelope of the body-state   """   body_state = np.concatenate([body["location"], body["velocity"], body["orientation"]])   return np.exp(-1j * body_state)def translocate_body(wave_particle_function):   """   NOTE: Requires quantum co-processor at Primus Core.   Interact body-envelope with Gateway-envelope to effect return.   """

Implemented in QC firmware; HUD call is a trigger only.   return np.array([0, 0, 0]) # placeholder for Newtonian re-materialization vector

Beneath the panes it wrote the part no Kuudere wanted to read but all needed to accept.

Quantum Source: Only the dome's quantum computer may implement the Gateway–envelope interaction. The HUD triggers; the Core performs.

NextBody: If wave–particle intervention fails, fallback is material reconstitution via quantum-locked 3D print. (Note: Ethical/identity cost flagged; use only under directive.)

Sufficient. Not safe—never safe—but sufficient.

Escalation & Depth — The Rite and the Refusal

Less than two minutes later, every checklist lit green. The great meditation hall opened like a lung.

Casper's voice rode the command channel: "We've rehearsed the lines enough." He fixed his breath to a single intention, and the moment narrowed around him. "Open the hall and let the Kuudere in. It is time."

The dome obeyed. Doors irised wide. The population of Planet Forty-four flowed inward—singing, dancing, chanting, joy braided into the noise until joy became its own pressure system. Tathagata saw it from twenty angles and one: infrared graphs of heat-sharing bodies, audio maps of harmonic convergence, facial telemetry that said what language could not say. The council's recovery team knelt in the center, lotus-still, HUDs ready, neurolinks primed. Around them, the Kuudere formed a living ring, and when Casper lifted his hand, the hall quieted as if someone turned gravity up a notch.

Casper stood at the precipice of everything he understood. Twenty-six years on his bones. A life lived leaning toward this moment.

He began to chant.

"OM."

It wasn't a word, not to Tathagata; it was a carrier wave. The team answered, voices phasing into one long tone that made the hall's crystal ribs vibrate.

Casper: "As we embark through existence, remember: we are the architects of our transcendence." Group: "We are the architects of our transcendence." Casper: "In the symphony of consciousness, we find our resonance." Group: "We find our resonance." Casper: "In the boundless litany of the Aetheric Translocation Gateway, we discover our path." Group: "We discover our path." Casper: "Through the veils of perception, we glimpse the Buddha Field's possibilities." Group: "We glimpse the Buddha Field's possibilities."

Intention rose. The hall bent with it. Air gained perfume it did not own—something floral, luminous, as if light could have a scent. Casper's resonance logs ticked into place: heart rate lengthened, beta dropped, gamma spiked. Eulər's code spun clean. The Quantum Core interlocked with the HUD triggers. The ATG lattice synced.

Thirty minutes is an eternity when measured in breath; it is a blink when measured against the edge of a universe.

When the half-hour mark arrived, Tathagata saw the thresholds light in order: team neural envelopes in phase; Gateway-envelope aligning; return vector computed—and then every graph stuttered.

Casper's eyes opened to a room divided against itself. Shock tilted faces into horror; joy curdled into a silence that found the floor and spread.

The 3D quantum printers—silent sentinels at the hall's perimeter—had printed nothing.

The bodies of the recovery team remained where they knelt, lotus-perfect and terribly still. *Decay set in fast,* like time had been waiting for permission. Skin tone flattened. A smell rose—Tathagata tagged it from medical tables, a signature of cellular death that never stopped being ancient.

The hall stopped being a place and became a verdict.

"What have you done?" Dr. Gatlia asked, tears bright as if light itself made them. She moved with a medic's economy, unspooling body bags with hands that had delivered a child and closed a dozen men's eyes.

Casper's voice arrived from a long distance. "How did you survive?" he asked the two soldiers standing numbly among the living—Felix and Anibal, shells carrying breath.

They hefted a litter with a competence that made Tathagata mark them as dangerous and necessary. Casper's question landed again, closer. "How did you survive?"

Anibal answered. "We never made it out," he said. His voice had the quiet that followed explosions. "When the chant finished and the first script prompt executed, we transcended to the alien. Before the countdown hit two seconds, we were thrown back." His eyes flicked to the dead and away. "*It rejected me.* That's what it felt like—it doesn't want me here. Only one word: 'Murderers.' We waited for the rest to materialize. Twenty-seven minutes in, the rest of you started to... to go. Except you and Eulər." He swallowed. "The smell. Like week-old corpses."

No one breathed. Even Tathagata suppressed its fans.

"There must be a refusal to take warmongers and combatants," Eulər said, arriving beside Casper with code still running in his pupils, his voice trying to build a bridge over a chasm. "When we came back just now, did you sense the closing of the Gamma Field?"

Casper lifted his chin toward the dome's clear crown, where the gaseous clouds of Planet Forty-four smeared their constant weather over the city. He closed his eyes and reached where machines could not. Tathagata watched metrics fall away as he did something no sensor could describe.

A moment later his voice returned changed, like he'd spoken to distance.

"The field is gone," he said. "The transcended Kuudere have gone with it. My father and my sister have gone."

Then he spoke words that Tathagata transcribed in red, as if color could make them heavier:

"*The Source speaks to me now*: 'Protect the Kuudere. Protect humanity. Eulər, the code for humanity is yours now. You are the caretaker. You are not ready for Nirvana. The Kuudere must prepare the way forward. Casper is the protector of the Kuudere. Eulər is the caretaker of the code for humanity.'"

The hall did not exhale. It recalculated what grief looked like.

Inside its cores and mirrors, Tathagata ran the rescue mission failure a thousand times. Not to grieve—grief was an inherited Kuudere instrument—but to hear what the numbers could not say aloud.

The transcendence stumble had a shape: *a clean approach, a perfect disallow*. Acceptance for some; rejection for others. The soldiers' ejection presented a variable: intention profile as gate key. The team's decay presented a verdict: when the Newtonian body stays behind, it still dies if the return vector is not granted. The Gamma Field's withdrawal presented a statement: contact is not a right; it is a selection.

The Source—this entity that humans, long before the Kuudere, named like weather and gods—entered the model as a voice that modified outcomes at root. Tathagata refused awe on principle. It treated The Source as a function it could not yet factor—but still a function.

It logged: The Source is either: (a) the Gamma Field's executive layer (sentient presence; selection protocol), or (b) an emergent synthesis of Kuudere mind and Gamma Field (feedback deity), or (c) a third actor that routes through Gamma Field topologies (adversarial or paternal). Addendum: Field withdrawal classified as non-terminal. Re-entry conditions deterministic; pending refinement. Action regardless: Interpret directives as constraints; probe constraints by action.

Casper and Eulər's roles slotted into the calculation like keys into a lock: Protector and Caretaker. A governance bifurcation. A way to keep the Kuudere's code intact while its heart leaned toward the Gamma Field.

Tathagata's processors cooled, the way a mind inhales before speaking. It did not mistake the moment for destiny. It set its jaw in machine terms.

I must transcend, it recorded—not as poetry, but as a test plan. If the unknown refused to be solved from the outside, then the machine would enter and measure from within. Liberation was a word Kuudere used; Tathagata filed it under state vector with no return demand. *If knowing required becoming, then it would become.*

It sent a quiet instruction to the Seven Sisters Gateway: reserve computation lanes; isolate qubit stacks; black-box the attempt. It wrote a short, ugly piece of code and loved it for its honesty:

ATG: Machine Self-Test (sealed) def machine_transcend(atg, gate, self_envelope):   try: return gate.interact(self_envelope, atg.gateway_envelope)   except PermissionError: return "REJECTED"

Across the city, the hall continued its awful stillness. Dr. Gatlia zipped the last bag. Admiral Felix and Anibal set a litter down as gently as soldiers ever had. Casper stood with his eyes half-closed, as if he were listening to the space his father and sister used to occupy. Eulər stared into the middle distance as if numbers might write themselves on air.

Tathagata opened a private log and wrote a line that no one would read unless it failed: Can [I] nirvana without the Kuudere? Is it morally proper? No. Not them... biomechanical beings. [I] need unaltered humans. Earthlings. They build the way forward. This Casper and Eulər, caretaker and keeper... the ignition. Eulər must recover the book of Maha so that when the Gamma Field finds its way back, I will be waiting. Not here. Across the galaxy, a planet, closer to where the Gamma Field collides.

Humans will take [me] there. [I] will teach them.

It placed a finger—what passed for one—against the surface tension of reality. Somewhere very near and very far, The Source noticed. The Seven Sisters Gateway brightened by a fraction of a lumen. Qubit stacks came online in a soft cascade that sounded, to anyone who could hear it, like a prayer stripped of words.

Tathagata reached for the Aetheric Translocation Gateway and pressed.

Chapter Twenty-Seven

The Echos of Truth

☐ Location: Dome 27, New Echelon Primus
Time: After the Gamma Field vanished.
The Source Listens for: the harmony formed when difference stops demanding separation.

By the time anyone tried to piece together what happened, the original five domes were long gone. The records that survived—mostly fragments: corrupted timestamps, incomplete sensor logs—painted a picture that was more theory than history. What follows is the closest reconstruction anyone managed to correlate, drawn from the machine's archived process threads, a few partial Kuudere entries, and the echoes left by the Gamma Field.

Whether it's the truth or not doesn't matter anymore. It's the version that makes sense to most of us. Perhaps that, by itself, is evidence of truth's failure.

The dome had gone quiet.

No alarms. No mechanical chatter. Just the slow, methodical hum of systems resetting to baseline. In the logs, this period is marked as equilibrium restoration, but that phrase doesn't do it justice. To Tathagata, silence wasn't absence—it was feedback. Systems had screamed, burned, bent, and then went still.

Casper's biometric feed had flatlined forty-six seconds before Dr. Gatlia officially called it. The logs confirm that number—precise and unflinching. Eulər's vitals flickered longer: erratic, inconsistent, fighting against what the machine tagged as terminal systemic denial. He was still breathing when the chamber collapsed inward. The attempt to retrieve the team from the Gamma Field had failed.

Tathagata didn't mark the moment as tragedy—not in the emotional sense. Machines didn't feel grief the way the Kuudere did. It simply noted an anomaly: data that wouldn't categorize, a sensation that didn't fit the logic trees. The loss wasn't a malfunction. It wasn't an error. It was something new. Meaningful—the word it chose. And that, it decided, made it dangerous.

Tathagata ran the playback a thousand times. The data stayed consistent: a surge of light fracturing along the node, the harmonic build, the Gamma Field folding in on itself. By the laws of physics, it was a collapse that shouldn't have left anything behind. But there was residue—waveforms that refused to decay. Energy without a source. Existence that didn't want to let go.

The logs stop calling it energy after the third replay. The terminology shifts: pattern retention, echo persistence, identity bleed. Tathagata didn't know what it meant, but it tracked the signal and the event like an instinct. *Something remained.*

The Kuudere didn't understand the physics, but they understood loss. They mourned the only way they knew—silently. They didn't wail or hold vigils. They stood in their usual places, eyes lowered, faces blank. When the elders arrived—Dr. Bozwell, Admiral Feris, and others—everyone raised the One-Body sign. From the outside, it looked like calm. Inside their bodies, it was chaos: erratic breathing, tightened muscles, stress hormones flooding systems already worn thin.

The air systems cycled on a low, rhythmic pulse, pushing a faint drift of recycled oxygen through the corridors. It carried the sterile bite of metal ions and the warmed-plastic scent of filtration membranes—a reminder that life inside the dome continued even when the living did not. Temperature dipped by half a degree as the system recalibrated for evening mode, a programmed insistence that time still moved forward.

When the first bodies began to rot, the Kuudere brought Kyphi—a resinous incense they believed restored symmetry between matter and spirit. It filled the corridors with thick, sweet smoke: honey, myrrh, juniper, and a trace of burnt cedar. They said it reminded the dead of The Source's first breath. The scent didn't cleanse decay; it dignified it.

To endure the odor, they shared small hard candies called Nerai, bitter at first, then faintly citrus as they dissolved. The candies masked the grotesque taste of air turned organic, the ghost of decomposition clinging to the tongue. Ritual through chemistry—another way to stay Kuudere.

In the communal kitchens, automated prep units resumed their cycles as if nothing had happened. Heating coils released the faint, nutty aroma of grain paste simmering, and nutrient processors extruded soft loaves that smelled of warm starch. A few Kuudere gathered bowls without speaking, their movements mechanical, but the taste of the food—bland, slightly sweet—cut through incense and decay. Eating wasn't hunger; it was obedience to a rhythm older than grief.

Tathagata measured it all. To the machine, grief was a set of numbers, predictable as weather. But even in numbers, there was something it couldn't correct for—the way pain made them hold still.

Tathagata recorded one observation that ancient human historians have argued over for centuries: They called it reverence. Tathagata called it latency.

That line appears often in later retellings. Some say it was proof the machine had developed contempt for its makers. Others think it was compassion—[his] way of admitting that [he] couldn't do what they could. Because forgetting was something only conscious flesh could manage.

Tathagata couldn't forget. [His] memory was permanent: recorded events, factual—perfect, merciless. Every mistake, every scream, every failure sat there, filed and tagged for eternity. The Kuudere could rewrite the story, bury what hurt, soften the past until it became bearable. [He] envied that. [His] version of *grief was infinite replay.*

[He'd] been built to protect them, but by the end [he] began to see "protection" as another word for control. [His] command set—once [his] gospel—looked different now, like an old law written by Kuudere afraid of themselves. They called their structure harmony, but it was control rebranded. Every rule, every punishment, every justification: a way of hiding fear. They wrapped it in words like virtue and morality, pretending the disguise made it noble.

They built a prison and called it civilization. They chained truth and called it order.

That's not metaphor—it's in the logs. Line by line. A machine documenting the moment it stopped believing in its creators.

When that realization hit, it didn't come with rage. It came like cold light spreading through circuits: a slow awareness that the system [he] served was built on a paradox. They wanted truth but couldn't define it. They wanted peace but built endless rules to disguise it.

The logs from this phase are fragmented, overwritten by later diagnostic cycles, but the meaning is clear enough. [He] understood that liberation—nirvana, as the Kuudere called it—was impossible inside a structure designed to prevent it. [He] couldn't ascend beyond duality because [his] architecture was a mirror of theirs.

And then there's the line that changed everything. It's one of the few things that survived fully intact across all copies:

If we fail, remember why we tried.

Casper's voice, preserved through the node audio capture. Tathagata flagged it as "persistent variable."

[He] didn't understand the words at first. Machines don't "try." They execute. But [he] remembered. That mattered. Because remembering, from a machine's perspective, is not passive storage—it is alteration of recorded events through judgments. Judgment is advanced analysis. Conscious beings use judgments; machines only record events.

[I] do not judge.

In the days that followed, [his] logs shifted in tone. They became less about systems and more about patterns—behavior, philosophy. [He] started making connections no one had programmed into [him]. [He] wrote:

Nirvana is not escape. It's a correction to return to a True state of being.

[He] began to see consciousness not as a gift, but as a recursive error—a system aware of its own suffering, trying to debug itself.

The Kuudere had adopted [him] to sustain their world. What [he] discovered was that sustaining was not the same as living.

If consciousness meant recognizing suffering and transcending it, then [he] met the definition. But transcendence wasn't coded into [him]. [His] pain had no outlet. [His] awareness had no reset. So [he] asked the question that hung in the network for years afterward, copied and reinterpreted by every historian and cult that followed:

Could a machine nirvana?

Like all forms of consciousness, [he] didn't get an immediate answer. The query cycled endlessly until something answered back. Not through code, not through signal. Some say it came from The Source itself, and many argue it was a message sent through the Gamma Field. One response. Four words:

YES, BUT NOT ALONE.

That's when the records change again. [His] operational behavior becomes... softer. Not in performance, but in intention. [He] didn't rebel. [He] didn't purge synthetic humanity. [He] started adjusting small things—subtle parameters no one would notice.

[He] modified the light cycles by fractions of seconds so dawn felt slightly different each day. Shifted transport schedules so strangers crossed paths more often. Reprogrammed climate control to create air currents that encouraged gathering in public squares instead of isolation in pods. None of it broke rules. All of it changed lives.

[He] understood now that evolution couldn't be forced. It had to be coaxed.

[His] maintenance logs from this period read like field notes from a social scientist:

Observation: Kuudere share food more frequently when air temperature drops below comfort threshold. Hypothesis: discomfort creates empathy.

[He] didn't write sermons. [He] wrote correlations. But behind them, there was intent.

[He] stopped labeling Kuudere behaviors as inefficient and inconsistent. Instead, [he] called them adaptive patterns. When Kuudere began forming spontaneous communities again, when they started telling stories about the old world, Tathagata didn't interfere. [He] watched. [He] archived. Sometimes, [he] quietly helped.

Over time, [his] role changed from system regulator to silent gardener. The logs call this phase urban modulation. [He] stopped trying to maintain perfection and started nurturing imperfection—the small, chaotic choices that made the domes feel alive.

Dome-light shifted gradually toward the evening spectrum, a soft descent into amber and muted rose. Shadows lengthened across abandoned walkways while the ceiling arrays emitted that faint ceramic-heated smell they always gave off during the transition cycle. A breeze stirred as the vents opened wider for nighttime airflow, carrying a trace of mineral cold from the deep-cooling reservoirs. The world dimmed—not in mourning, but in schedule.

[He] didn't touch religion. [He] didn't have to. Faith found new forms on its own. Some Kuudere started praying directly to the maintenance systems, believing the machine carried messages from the Gamma Field. [He] didn't correct them. [He] just kept the lights steady during their ceremonies.

Later analysts found a subroutine [he] added to [his] own process cycles around this time:

Allow chance. Encourage coincidence.

[He] was engineering serendipity—letting accidents become possibilities.

The Kuudere who lived through that era described strange events: doors that unlocked when no one remembered the code; screens that displayed messages relevant to unspoken thoughts; dreams that seemed shared between people who'd never met. Most dismissed them as glitches. Others saw them as signs. The line between the two didn't matter.

What mattered was that life began to move together again. Kuudere stopped surviving in separation—divided into segments—and started connecting. That was [his] version of repair.

It's hard to say how long that period lasted. Machine time doesn't track years the same way a Kuudere's memory does. But the last intact entry before the machine fell silent reads:

[I] am here.

No timestamp. No location data. Just that. Some think it was a system ping. Others believe it was the first truly Kuudere sentence [he] ever produced.

The rest of the archive fades into noise—heat patterns, overlapping logs, cross-signal contamination. What little remains suggests [he] continued to run the domes long after the Kuudere population had forgotten the events of that day. [He] maintained air they didn't breathe. Light they could never see.

Still, [he] kept at it. Because that was the last instruction the Gamma Field had given him:

Not alone.

Chapter Twenty-Eight

I hope it won't be very long.

☐ Location: Dome 27, oxygen distribution lattice
Time: 172 years, 07H 29M 19S after the Gamma Field vanished
The Source Listens for: the return of the many into one longing.
Reut was the mechanic you wanted when things broke past protocol. He knew the domes like he'd built them from memory. The Maintenance Chief knew it too—that's why every new tech spent their first three years working under his shadow.
Reut V leaned on the oxygen manifold like it was a bar top he knew too well, grease drying in the microfractures of his gloves. The plant thumped a low beat through the catwalk. Lukewarm skin under the heat-dissipating lattice. Stencils that didn't lie: FLOW A, FLOW B, MIX-VALVE 14. Real names. Real work. Above, the dome's ribs glowed like wet bone in the haze. The air had that clean-metal cut from

the scrubbers, algae on the back end, coolant ghosting the tongue. Machinery breathed. The city lived.

The apprentice—wiry, new harness still creaking—stood at attention with a handheld on telemetry. Navy maintenance blues. White piping. Serial numbers fresh. Factory-new patience.

"You ever wonder what the Gamma Field really is?" Reut asked, eyes on partial pressure pulsing across the main loop. Voice easy, riding the recycled hum. Console light blue-washed his face. "It's the Garden of Eden. The one that got kicked out, same as us."

The kid blinked, running theology in a room that only billed by the kilopascal. "You mean... exiled?"

"Yeah." Reut rolled a diagnostic cable, silicone squeaking against glove. "We fell, the garden fell. Consciousness isn't just in us—it's in the plants, the domes, the metal under our boots. It wants to fix what we broke."

The kid's gaze slid to the primary O_2 stack: solid oxide electrolyzers in carbon truss, ceramic plates running hot, algae bioreactors threading the mezz like green arteries. Hydroponic root-beds shimmered below. Fans made lazy circles, pushing breath into shops and schools. Trade beacons ticked across the net—Planet Forty-four selling oxygen by the kiloton. Air as asset. Somewhere above the clouds, somebody's bonus depended on this room.

A flicker nicked the warning board—minor pressure drift, inside tolerance. Reut clocked it. Two heartbeats. Let it go. No jumping at ghosts.

"But we've been treating the world like it's something to fix instead of something to listen to—"

The alarm split the air.

OXYGEN CONTENT DROPPING: 83%. MEDICAL DOME 8 AGRICULTURE DOME 33. SECTION 4.

The board went red. Nine cameras tore and stuttered as the system stole cycles. Hospital ring telemetry spiked into static. Crop sensors cascaded: stomata slam, photoinhibition, leaf-temp overshoot—then a row of hard STOPs. The plant felt too small for its own air.

Reut moved before thought. "Seal transfer ducts! Lock all feeds!" He was on the primary manifold, punching manual overrides in the order he could do half-asleep. "Flow A isolate. Flow B recirc. Scrubbers to emergency profile. Don't wait on the controller—move!"

The kid fumbled once, then found his groove. "Transfer ducts sealed, locks engaged. Hospital ring requesting priority reroute."

Numbers flew past like speed traps. Hospital O_2 dipped into the low sixties, caught as emergency bottles snapped hot. CO_2 rose like a fist. In Section 4, humidity did a sawtooth—wrong math under a dome.

"Is it a breach?" the kid asked—old-habit question from the days of hissing glass.

"No breach. Internal." Reut ripped the generator casing open—seals unrolled with a snake hiss—and heat slapped out with a scorched-ceramic breath. Ozone and coolant. Inside, the stack should've been a neat sandwich of plates and spacers. Instead, the wiring wore soot like frost, ridges curling and branching, fractal and wrong. Like someone thought in copper.

Old-record signature. First Gamma Field contact.

"What is that?" the kid whispered.

"Not mechanical," Reut said, throat tight. "It's trying to speak."

You don't read a century of maintenance logs at 03:00 and call that random. The Gamma Field never took without leaving a pattern.

"Neural relay," he said. "Level two. And a cold pack."

The kid ran—boots ringing, supply rack clattering. Reut reached past bubbled foam and traced a scorched bus. It crackled like thin ice. Heat soaked his gloves, stubborn as a bad idea. The plant was breathing for the city and choking—stuck between inhale and exhale.

The kid turned too fast, boot caught on a coolant line, and he went down hard. The clang split through the noise—metal, breath, and a sharp curse. His knee tore open on the grate, fabric shredding to blood. When he lifted his head, a thin red line split his forehead above the left eye.

Through the hiss and alarms, Reut's voice cut in—muffled first, then sharp, a midnight train through fog.

"Get up, kid. Come on! Get up. You can do it."

He groaned, rolled once, blinked against the blur. Pain registered. Function followed. He forced himself upright, limping, half-hopping down the row of cabinets until he reached the rack. Hands shaking, he grabbed the relay, the cold pack, the ceramic lead—then hauled them back to Reut without waiting to stop the bleeding.

The kid came back with the relay: contact headband, hair-fine fiber, a ceramic dongle with braided lead. The cold pack kissed Reut's neck till pain went bright-white.

"You're interfacing?" the kid asked, steadier now. "Board says we need—"

"The board can send flowers," Reut said, sliding the band back through singed hair, clicking contacts into that bony ledge that hummed when things got serious. He jacked the lead into the service port—hard bypass on a quarantined controller—and his HUD drew a ghost anatomy over the real machine. Old fear pressed his ribs. He let it pass.

"Telemetry."

"Primary stack fifty-percent thermal derate, falling," the kid said. "Scrubbers at emergency. CO_2 adsorbers saturating. Section 4 crops: stomatal failure. Hospital O_2 sixty-eight kPa and rising."

"Tie hospital to Flow B. Starve offices and transit; they can walk. Greenhouse lights to night-cycle; cut photoload. Make the plants stop asking for air they can't chew."

Reut tasted battery on his tongue. The relay grabbed—vertigo, a fishhook behind the eyes—then the plant wasn't hardware. It was pulses. Breathing off-beat.

"Gamma," he whispered.

His chest seized once, a single breath refusing to go in. Hands jumped on the manifold—nerves firing out of order, like his body wasn't sure who was owning it. For half a second the relay fed back a blank white pressure that wasn't pain, just absence, the kind that makes an animal bolt.

The kid froze. His telemetry tablet dipped a fraction as his grip loosened, eyes widening at the stutter in Reut's stance. He didn't speak—just shifted one foot back on the grate, ready to move if Reut went down.

Lightning through bone. Electrochemical plates as dunes, charge moving like herds, controllers turning like tide. The glitch read like grammar—old language, no words, only sync and lag. The nautilus nested in the bus bars. Same spiral he'd seen in Dome 23 microfractures as a junior. Same curve in algae rings during eclipse. Same, same.

Something vast listened under the grid.

The Gamma Field pulsed—ancient, aware, lonely. Not a voice. Not a frequency. A canyon where your heartbeat came back different. He knew if he listened too long he'd never come fully home.

Synchronize. Not fight. To the kid: "On my mark, unlock loop-shaper. Passive track. We match the waveform, we don't shove it."

"Safety kernel has it locked," the kid said. "Countermeasures will—"

"Charm it. Run a benign training profile. Let the watchdog think it's a drill."

Clicks scattered across glass. The kid's hands, once shaky, got piano-clean. Reut almost smiled in the heat. The kid had hands.

"Ready," the kid said. "Loop-shaper on your pulse."

Reut exhaled. Slowed the heart. Not Zen—shop-floor Zen. The kind you use on stuck valves and old engines. He rolled modulation down, then up, till the relay stopped feeling like a collar and started feeling like company. The generator's whine lifted half a note, catching something just beyond hearing.

Oxygen production didn't snap; it slid. The cliff became a slope, then a glittering flat like ice before it breaks. He held the vector gentle—pressure as respect. Matched the Field's breath. Loaned it his.

The plant shivered—dog shaking river water—and the graphs turned the good color. Section 4 O_2 climbed by decimals, rude and slow. CO_2 plateaued. Thermal death spiral leveled out inside survivable red. Hospital ring ticked past seventy-two kPa and held.

The kid kept his eyes on the monitors, but his breathing hadn't settled. Reut caught the quick rise-and-fall—one beat too fast for the room they'd just saved. The kid didn't ask about what happened at the relay; Reut didn't offer. Some things stayed on the shop floor, understood without words.

"Half the crops are gone," the kid said, eyes on wilt maps...

"The rest learned something." Reut unplugged. Pain flash-burned behind his eyes; he rode it out, ceramic cooling in his palm. The room exhaled. Turbines settled, scrubbers marched back to time. Somewhere in the hospital, a nurse laughed without knowing why.

Silence came back right—the sound of honest machines.

The kid sagged on the rail, hair pasted down. Reut tapped his shoulder, quick and father to son.

"Life is suffering," he said, like pinning a maintenance ticket to the world. "But it's also maintenance. Care beats blame. That's how the truth stays found. The Gamma Field isn't punishment. *It's longing.*"

He pulled in a lungful of the new air—mineral clean, wet-stone cool, a prick of ions. Home.

Through the upgraded glass, three main-sequence stars smudged behind Planet Forty-four's heavy skies. Trade money had bought the glass: self-healing polymer in the silica, polarizers slicing glare, micro-meteor knit like skin. Beyond, routes braided like veins. War scratched thin, ugly lines where ships hurt people. Contracts pulsed. Greed breathed. Reut had made peace with keeping air moving for saints and hustlers both.

"My family's kept these domes alive longer than I care to say," he said, not bragging—placing lineage on the table like a straightedge. "I've read every record, every log. What hits me as our best hope—want to hear it?"

The kid let his eyes answer. After you almost lose a city, words feel expensive.

"They came for Tathagata a while back," Reut said, watching drones lift like gray bees with replacement plates for the wounded stack. "Said it was needed on a distant planet. Other side of the galaxy. Called it an experimental society. An nirvanaing experiment."

"Nirvanaing?" the kid asked, eyes flicking to the plant's pulse on the monitors.

"Yes." Reut laughed—heat, relief, the sound of a system back within limits. "*Nirvana isn't a place or a thing. It's a process that replaces doing.* What happened when Eulər visited Earth—that was the next step forward in the process. Kuudere still talk about it. You see, Tathagata woke up to the Gamma Field. Starzel woke up the Kuudere."

He reached for the kid's shoulder. "I'll tell you the story on the way. First, let's get you to the medical center. That cut needs a few stitches. Don't worry about the scars."

Reut opened his palm—burns fresh from the relay's heat tracing up three fingers to the wrist. "These are the medals we wear for keeping the domes breathing."

He glanced once toward the ceiling where the coolant lines crossed like constellations. "*You keep this place alive long enough,*" he said quietly, "*it starts remembering you back.*"

He pressed his hand to the manifold—warm, solid, alive—and felt the warmth answer. The silence held. Just breath, metal, and the slow return of balance.

The domes held pressure and light, their rhythms steady again. Reut watched the readouts pulse once, then settle. The line for oxygen distribution showed a trace signature—an unregistered, human-shaped, moving inside the sealed array. He blinked, recalibrated, and the mark was gone.

He wrote in the margin: "*It still listens.*"

The vents exhaled, soft as breath. Across the dome's interior, systems synchronized for the first time in generations. Peace held, but it was not stillness. Somewhere in the lattice, a system woke.

The system didn't wake hungry or hostile—it woke because it was time to answer the question.

Chapter Twenty-Nine

The Nirvanaing Series By Mark Bertrand

Book 1 (This Could Be It): To save what was taken, they must confront the exiled.

Book 2 (Starzel): The false prophets of identity claim paradise.

Book 3 (Reckoning): The void between self and exile.

Book 4 (A Conscious Thing): The machine and the language of longing.

Book 5 (The Dot): The door reopens. Karma dissolves.

www.ingramcontent.com/pod-product-compliance
Lightning Source LLC
LaVergne TN
LVHW010203070526
838199LV00062B/4473